A KIND OF PRISONER

THE DEPARTMENT Z SERIES

A KIND OF PRISONER

DEPARTMENT Z

JOHN CREASEY

OPEN ROAD

INTEGRATED MEDIA

NEW YORK

ISBN: 978-1-5040-9270-8

This edition published in 2024 by Open Road Integrated Media, Inc.
180 Maiden Lane
New York, NY 10038
www.openroadmedia.com

A KIND OF PRISONER

1

HOMECOMING

J udy Ryall heard the ring at the front door bell as she was
moving from the kitchen to the sitting-room of the flat.
She stopped in the tiny hall. The only light came from the
sitting-room, but the door was nearly closed, and in the hall it
was very dull.

It wasn't a long, steady ring; just brief and halfhearted, as if
someone had touched the bell and then snatched a finger
away.

Judy stood listening, her heart thumping.

Fear was an ugly thing; and by night it had become her
constant companion. She could not fully understand it. It
came whenever Alec was away. He was now, on another of his
mysterious errands. She hated it. She hated his being away,
but more than anything she hated the fear which crept upon
her with the night's darkness. She knew of no reason for it;
she tried to laugh at it, but could only hold it at bay during
daylight. It always came on the wings of the dusk.

The bell did not ring again, but there was an unfamiliar

sound; a panting sound. She could picture a dog, lying down after a long, exciting run; that was it, someone was panting.

Then she heard a different sound; the faintest ting at the bell, it could hardly be called a ring. Then came tapping, not sharp or hard, but muffled and slow. The panting came, also.

Then came a voice: "Judy," a man whispered, as if in pain: "Judy."

That was—Alec. Her husband; gasping the word.

Fright paralysed the muscles of Judy's mouth and her lips; and when she tried to move, her body seemed to resist. But she had to open the door now. She could just see the dark shape of the electric light switch. She stretched out a hand, and forced herself to go forward until she could touch it.

Light flooded the tiny hall, but brought no real relief, for at the same moment came another short, sharp ring at the bell; another hoarse: "Judy." She felt icily cold. She was close enough to open the door, now, but her muscles seemed dead. The panting noise continued, but the tapping had stopped and Alec didn't call out again.

She heard a thud, against the door.

"No!" she screamed, and with the cry there came some release from the paralysing fear. She slid the knob back and pulled the door wide, ready to scream again. But she did not.

Alec stood there.

Alec, her husband, Alec her lover and beloved, stood with the light shining on a face so pale that all the blood might have been drained from it. His eyes were huge, dark, filled with pain. He leaned against the side of the door, and his right hand was stretched out. He was gasping for breath; panting.

"Alec," she breathed, and there was no scream now, because of his desperate need. She took his arm, to draw him into the room. "Come in, and—"

He resisted her, and without being told, she knew that it

4

was with a great effort. He licked his lips; he looked as if he might fall dead at her feet.

"Judy—ring this—number. Say you're my wife. Give the man—"

He stopped, but his lips kept working; it was as if the words he wanted wouldn't come. He stood with his huge pain-racked eyes and his desperately pale face, resisting his wife with one arm, and thrusting the other forward—with the envelope in it. It brushed against her hand.

"Give the man—who comes—this. Don't—don't open—"

He stopped again.

He turned his head—and sounds outside became clearer; footsteps.

Something happened to Alec. He thrust the envelope into Judy's hand, somehow compelling her fingers to close over it. Then he pushed her away. She couldn't resist, just staggered back. He did not look as if he had the strength, but there was no resisting his pressure.

"Lock, bolt, door." His voice suddenly became powerful. "Shut—"

He stretched forward, grabbed the door and closed it before she could move. It slammed. The bell gave a sharp ting. There were strange sounds outside, of movement and of voices. She shot the lower bolt, as a key scraped in the lock. The door shook but didn't open. Soon there came a long, urgent ring of the bell.

Alec had vanished; in his place was the solid wooden door, with the battery of the bell inside; and the bolts top and bottom.

Judy wanted to open the door, call Alec, help him, save him; but she did not. The bell rang again. She knew that there was desperation in Alec's mind, that although he might be dying, he was desperately anxious for her to do what he told her; he wanted that more than anything else in the world. She had known for a long time that he held his work more dear than life. Work—service. Mysterious, deadly, sinister secret service. This had begun the fear in her, vague at first until tonight; there was all the justification for fear.

All the horrors she had imagined had become real.

The bell jarred out again.

She put out a hand and shot the top bolt. She hardly knew what she was doing; she was not thinking beyond the words of his instructions, which she would never forget. She felt that they were the last words that he would ever speak to her, that obeying them was a trust.

She looked at the envelope.

It was just an ordinary cream-laid one, sealed, and with no address. At the top was scrawled a telephone number:

Whitehall 08181

Judy could hear that husky voice, hear words which had been uttered as if with the last effort he would ever be able to make.

". . . ring this—number. Say you're my wife. Give the man—who comes—this. Don't—don't open—"

That was all, before the sounds had come from the stairs.

The bell rang again and there was a thud at the door; Judy knew that whoever was there would try to break it down. The light of the hall was bright upon her as she turned towards the living-room. Her mouth was dry, her face seemed stiff, her eyes were wide open, rounded, as if she couldn't close them. There was the warm, comfortable room, with the pictures which Alec had chosen and the precious things that they shared, and on the other side of the fireplace her chair, with the work-basket by its side, the light glinting on a pair of scissors.

The telephone was by Alec's big, winged chair.

"Ring this—number."

She looked down at it again, while the ringing at the door and the thudding stopped; and that seemed more ominous than the noise itself. *Whitehall* 08181. She actually lifted the receiver and began to dial, when a sound came at the window.

She screamed, dropped the telephone, turned. She gaped at the billowing curtains, at the man behind them and the open window. Fear worse than she had ever known held her in a vice. She could not move, could only stand with her mouth open, the telephone hanging from its platform, the letter in her hand.

The man jumped into the room, lithely; and landed as lightly and easily as a cat.

He smiled.

She had never seen him before. There was nothing remarkable about him; he was a little smaller than average, lean, youthful, hatless, wearing a brown coat. The thing which made him different was his smile. It wasn't at all sinister. At first it had no effect on Judy, except a negative one; it did nothing to worsen her fears. Then he turned his back on her, as the wind howled in. An ash-tray fell off a table, two photographs collapsed on the top of bookshelves on either side of the fireplace. As the window closed, calmness seemed to come into the room.

"Sorry to scare you, Mrs. Ryall," he said. He had a pleasant voice, and the remarkable thing was that his manner was so normal; somehow, he calmed her. "Sorry about it all. But we need your help." He smiled again, differently, as if trying to give her a message which words couldn't quite convey. "Alec would ask for it, too."

"Alec—" she began, and felt her body relaxing; it was almost as if the ice which had frozen in her veins was beginning to melt. "He—"

"I know, he's outside," the man said. "We'll do all we can. Did he give you this?" He moved towards her, but didn't take the letter. "And ask you to telephone Whitehall 08181?"

She found that she could answer. "Yes." His knowledge gave her confidence that this man was a friend of Alec. Afterwards she realised that there was no way of being sure, and that he might have fooled her; but at the moment she felt quite certain.

"May I?" He took it from her.

Another sharp ring came at the front door. It made Judy jump, brought fear back. But the man glanced calmly towards the door and didn't move.

"Impatient people," he said lightly. "They'll force it, soon. Mrs. Ryall, there's no time to explain, all I can say is that Alec would have wanted you to do this." He took another sealed envelope from his pocket—as the sounds grew louder outside. He ignored these, but scrawled the telephone number on this envelope, and handed it to her.

"Open the front door as soon as I've gone. Say this is what Alec gave you. Put up a fight." He kept smiling in that comforting way, although what comfort could anyone give her? "Make everything hard to get. We'll do all we possibly can to help Alec."

"Who—are you?"

"A colleague of Alec's," the man said. He was at the telephone, listening. "They've cut the wire. Better say you tried to ring the number on the envelope but couldn't get an answer. Will you?"

"I—I'll try, but—"

"I'll be seeing you," the man said. "Tuck that letter some-

8

where out of sight first." His eyes smiled. He stood by her side for a moment, gripping her wrist; his hand was strong, cool, steady. "Good luck, Mrs. Ryall. Fool 'em. Alec would want it."

He moved towards the window.

The scratching sounds were still audible at the front door.

The man pushed the window up, climbed out, then called almost in a whisper:

"Close it after me."

He stood up on the sill. This was the first floor, and there was a fall of thirty feet to concrete below; but he stretched up as if there were nothing at all to fear. He must have gripped something, for he pulled himself up. The curtains billowed in again, and all Judy could see were the man's legs; next his feet; then there was just the pitch darkness of the blustery night and the red curtain.

She closed the window, and turned round. She listened, but could no longer hear sounds at the door.

She had the second letter in her hand, stared at it, then moved suddenly and tucked it into the neck of her white blouse.

There were men outside whom Alec had wanted to outwit.

Her mind was hopelessly confused, but certain things made sense. Alec would want her to do what the unknown man had said; she had either to accept that or reject it, and she accepted it. She had to play for time; mustn't give the letter up at once. She had no idea who would come in, was simply certain that someone would.

She pulled back the bolts and the door opened.

Although she had been sure that it would, it set her heart beating wildly. Yet nothing in the appearance of the man who stood there need frighten. He was older than the one who had come in by the window, taller, rather gracious and almost benevolent looking. His hair was iron grey. He moved smoothly, and he smiled freely; but somehow there was no reassurance in his smile.

Another man was behind him.

"Stay there," this first man said to his companion and half closed the door before he approached Judy. She stood absolutely still, lips parted. "There's no need to be alarmed, Mrs. Ryall," the man went on. "Your husband will be all right—*if* you are helpful."

He smiled again and proffered cigarettes from a gold case—and intuitively, as she had trusted the other man, Judy felt savage hatred towards this one.

2

HARD TO GET

J udy didn't speak and didn't take the cigarette. The man took one without looking down at the case; put it slowly to his lips, then replaced the case in his pocket. With the same slow, deliberate movements, he took out a lighter.

"You'll both be all right, if you're helpful," he said. "And if you're not—"

He smiled again.

It was like a nightmare; as if all the fears Judy had lived with had taken possession of her sleep. But this was real. The man was real. And his smile was—frightening. It was worse because he obviously meant it to be reassuring; something of the very nature of evil seemed to show in his face, although it was handsome, and the expression was calm.

"I don't—I don't understand you," she said huskily.

"We can soon put that right," the man said. "Perhaps I should introduce myself—I am Malcolm Wright. Your husband may have spoken of me."

She moistened her lips.

"No."

"So he didn't discuss his cases with you?"

"He—no."

"Never?"

"No."

The man who called himself Malcolm Wright smiled again, as if smugly satisfied.

"He was very wise. I don't want to make this any more unpleasant than I can help, Mrs. Ryall, but earlier this evening he stole a letter from me. I want it back."

She had to say something; her mind was working at last, she was beginning to look beyond this moment to what might follow.

"I—I don't believe it!" She moved forward suddenly, hands clenched and raised. He backed away, momentarily startled. She shouted: "Where's Alec? What have you done to him? Where is he?"

"Now don't get excited." The man who called himself Wright took her wrists; he wasn't going to stand any nonsense. When he smiled again, Judy understood something of the difference between his smile and the first visitor's. This man's eyes were dull, cold; the other's had gleamed. "Getting excited won't help," Wright went on. "I'll help your husband if you behave yourself. He stole that letter and brought it here."

"He didn't!"

"Oh, yes, he did," said the man who wanted her to know him as Malcolm Wright, "and I want it, my dear. If you make too much trouble, you'll get hurt."

He meant that.

She could feel a corner of the envelope pressing into her. She had been asked not to give it up too easily, and felt certain that she must obey, but one thing was more important; helping Alec.

Could she?

For a moment she had believed that she had seen him alive for the last time; had felt that he would never speak to her again. Now hope surged back—hope, and the possibility that this man wasn't lying, that he could help Alec.

"Alec wouldn't—steal," she said. It was nonsense. Obviously Secret Service work might make him steal, but she had to say something.

"Mrs. Ryall," said Wright softly, "I want you to understand clearly that your husband stole this letter and that I know he brought it here. He was followed. He has been nowhere else. His car is outside, and has already been searched. He arrived here less than five minutes before us. He was in a state of collapse in the passage. We heard the door slam as we came into the hall downstairs. You are here alone; there is no one else to whom he could have given the letter. So—" he held out his hand. "Where is it?"

"I—I haven't got a letter!" She backed away. At least her mind was working, that gave some relief from numbing tension. "He—he must have dropped it on the way, he—"

"Do you *want* to get hurt?" Wright asked softly.

She didn't answer.

There was little chance of help.

This house stood in its own extensive grounds. A long drive led from the road, which was out of sight. The ground floor flat was to let, the flat above was usually occupied by a family now on holiday. The nearest neighbour was a quarter of a mile away. Beyond was the suburb of Barnes; the Thames; and not far off the sprawling mass of London.

If this man wanted to hurt her she couldn't stop him; screaming for help would be useless. He knew that; his smile said so, but it didn't really matter. She wanted only one thing; to find out whether Alec was alive, whether there was any way to help him.

"Where is Alec?" she asked, and caught her breath.

"He'll be all right, if—"

"Where is he?" she screamed, and jumped forward again. That was partly for effect, partly because her taut nerves were at breaking point. *"I want to see Alec, where is he?"*

Wright said smoothly: "He was badly hurt and we had to send him to a doctor, but he'll be all right, provided you give me the letter."

"I must see Alec," she cried. "I must—"

Wright moved. She hadn't time to evade his grasp. He snatched her wrist and then twisted her round, so that her back was towards him, her arm forced upwards behind her back.

"Kip!" he called.

Judy couldn't move. Her body was erect, rigid. The door opened wider and another man came in.

"Scarf," Wright said abruptly.

That meant something to the man he called Kip; next moment it meant plenty to Judy. Kip was small, inches shorter than Judy, just an ordinary little man. He took a white silk scarf out of his pocket, moved towards her, and wound the scarf round her face. He tied it tightly, with the knot against her teeth; her mouth was forced open all the time, she could hardly breathe.

Wright let her go.

"Start looking for it," he said.

Judy staggered towards a chair and dropped on to the arm of it; *Alec's.* She watched the two men shifting everything from the bureau; from the shelves; going through books, lifting cushions. They were very quick but thorough.

Five minutes passed . . .

Ten . . .

Wright, whose movements were all so smooth and carefully made, turned towards her. He was almost breathtakingly handsome, could look almost benevolent; no one passing him in the street was likely to get that impression of evil.

The man named Kip was turning up the corners of the carpet; he finished the fourth, and then moved towards Judy. He grinned. He had thin features, a nose with a red tip, and one eye looked larger than the other. She noticed his large hands too—much larger than Wright's, knuckly, ugly. He didn't untie the scarf but something pleased him. He moved suddenly; and Judy realised that a corner of the envelope showed at the V of her blouse.

The little man snatched the letter out with fingers which were icy cold, and handed it to Wright.

Wright seemed to stop breathing.

Judy sensed how much it mattered to him now—how desperately important it was. He held the letter for a moment and ripped it open.

It was a fake . . .

If he recognised that, the man who had come in at the window would fail. It mattered desperately that he shouldn't.

Wright read one sheet hurriedly then looked at another. His eyes lit up, satisfaction showed plainly.

Relief made Judy feel weak.

The scarf bit into her lips, and she was almost glad that it was there to stop her from smiling in that brief triumph.

"All right," Wright said. "We've got it."

"S'good." The small man watched Judy from narrowed eyes. His eyes told her a great deal; in some ways she felt more frightened of him than of the other. He rubbed his big hands together; big, ugly hands.

"Let's go," he said.

"What about the lady?" asked Wright smoothly.

"Well, what about her?"

"She's seen us," Wright said.

At first that did not mean anything to Judy. They were just words. Then she realised that they startled Kip, made him look at her with a different expression. All her fears came flooding back.

"We mustn't forget that, must we, Kip?" Wright said. "She's seen us, and that means she could recognise us again, doesn't it?"

"She won't talk," Kip growled, "not if she knows that her Alec will be killed if she does."

"Won't she?" asked Wright. "Can we rely on her?" He paused, then said abruptly: "Put her with Ryall, we can deal with them together."

Shock and pain went through her.

She had believed Alec was dead; then she had hoped; now she felt the truth beyond all doubt. Alec was dead. These men could look at her, too, and contemplate killing her—and Wright could say: "Put her with Ryall, we can deal with them together."

The scarf was tight about her lips. She couldn't make a sound and even if she could have screamed and cried and shouted, none but these two could have heard. She stood up from the chair, thrusting her hands out as if she could fend them off; but she felt quite sure that they were going to kill her. The one thing she didn't know was how.

"Okay," Kip said, "I'll fix her."

He moved towards her, just a little, prancing brute of a man, with his long arms and big hands hanging by his sides. Wright just watched.

Kip was very close.

Judy thrust her hands, palms outwards, towards him. She glanced at Wright, trying to appeal to him with her eyes, believing that death was near, and wanting so desperately to live. He watched her without moving, and his eyes were cold.

"It won't hurt," Kip said. "Much."

He moved his right hand in a slapping motion at her cheeks, and intuitively she moved her hands so as to protect her face. Promptly he thrust both hands out, those big, ugly hands with the knuckly fingers. Judy felt them grab at her throat, felt them grip and bury themselves in the flesh . . . She could not breathe.

She could not move; and suddenly she seemed to drop out of life. She did not know that she slumped back in the chair, or that Wright had called out sharply, or that they both went towards the window. Outside, bright headlights shone against the wall of the house from two cars.

"Think this is Craigie's men?" Kip asked, and he sounded nervous.

Wright didn't answer but reached the front door first, with the small man just behind him. It was dark on the landing and the staircase. They hurried down to the front hall. The car engines outside were switched off, but there were voices. As they neared the front door the bell rang.

"Must—must be Craigie's men," Kip muttered. His voice wasn't steady.

"We'll go out by a window," Wright said without answering. "Get a room door open."

Kip used a picklock, and had the door of the downstairs flat open in a few seconds. They went into the room beyond as a knock came at the front door.

3

CRAIGIE

The man who had climbed in at the window of the Ryalls'
flat turned off Whitehall on that blustery night in
March, and parked his car some distance along a narrow road.
He did not get out immediately, but waited, watching in the
mirror, making sure that no one had followed him.

Satisfied, he got out.

On the other side of the road, some distance from where
he left the car, was a small doorway. Every hour, hundreds of
people passed the end of this street and this doorway; but very
few ever noticed the door itself, fewer still approached it.

This man did.

He had a key, used it, and stepped inside a hallway which
had a dim yellow light. The door closed automatically, and he
heard the click as the lock shot home. Now all was quiet, all
sound of blustering was cut off. Facing the man was a flight of
stone steps.

He smiled faintly as he went up these; in fact the smile was
little more that a twist of his full lips, and did not really touch
his eyes. He went up to the second landing, then held the

handrail that was fastened to the blank wall. He knew exactly where to find the tiny crack beneath the handrail, large enough for him to insert a fingernail.

He did so and pressed.

Then he went up to the landing and stood outside what appeared to be a blank wall, distempered green. After a few seconds this began to open. There was a sliding door, with the join in a corner quite invisible. When it was open wide enough for the man to step through, it stopped. He went through and found himself—as he had known he would—in a small square cubicle.

The door closed behind him.

He now knew that he was being scrutinised through a glass window which prevented him from seeing into the room beyond. He knew also that when he was identified, one of the men—or perhaps the only man—inside would press a green button, set in a desk or in the mantelpiece; then another door would slide open for the visitor to pass through.

It all happened as it had to him a hundred times.

His smile widened.

Sitting in a winged armchair in front of a big carved oak fireplace, which had a bright coal fire, was a small man in his shirtsleeves. His feet were up on the mantelpiece, a meer- schaum with a light brown bowl dropped from his lips.

This was Gordon Craigie.

He fitted the chair; in fact he fitted the room, no one who ever came there felt that the room was as it should be without Craigie either in that chair or at one of three desks at the far end of the room. He was a fixture; almost as timeless as infinity.

"Hallo, Jim," Craigie said. "Come and sit down." He did not take the big pipe from his lips but pointed lazily to a chair. He might have been anything from fifty to sixty. His sparse grey hair was brushed straight back from a high forehead. He looked tired. No one who came in here knew what it was like to see Craigie unless he were tired. His eyes were perpetually weary yet had a certain brightness and good humour; he looked like a man who never had enough sleep.

James Merrick sat down.

He was still smiling faintly, and his eyes had now caught the smile which had impressed Judy.

"What's funny?" asked Craigie.

The smile turned into a grin.

"The whole set-up, Gordon," Merrick said. "Sometimes it gets too much for me. Sliding doors, secret panels, green lights, all the paraphernalia of melodrama. *And* it works. We ought to laugh it to death, but it won't be laughed at. Do you ever leave this room?"

Craigie took the meerschaum from his mouth.

"Occasionally. What's the matter with it?"

Merrick shrugged and glanced round. At this end it might have been a bachelor's living-room, with the easy chairs, the big cupboard with its door ajar and a few oddments poking out; the pipe-racks fastened to the wall; the big red clay jar of tobacco on top of the television set; a dozen and one things which stamped it as a room seldom touched by a woman. In contrast with the other end it was almost ludicrous; for the three desks were of green painted steel, with several telephones on each; there were filing cabinets, and a dictaphone on a wheeled stand. As the one end was homely and comfortable, the other might have been a business efficiency expert's office.

"Everything," Merrick said. "And nothing. Forget it. Any news?"

"No."

Merrick said: "Pity. I hope our chaps weren't too late."

"Who went to Ryall's place?"

"Corlett."

"Oh," Merrick said.

He sat down in a small armchair opposite Craigie. The fire warmed his knees. He took out a silver cigarette-case, lit a cigarette, stared into the fire, and then slowly took the envelope out of his pocket and handed it to Craigie.

"I hope it was worth sacrificing Alec," he remarked.

The words seemed to hurt.

Craigie took it, hesitated, then opened it. Thin papers, filled with pencilled lettering and figuring, were inside. He held each sheet up to the light, and then said: "It's all right, they haven't touched it. We're off to a good start."

The room fell silent but for their breathing and the rustle of coals settling in the fire; it was a painful silence, and Merrick found himself looking at the one telephone by Craigie's side, on a small table. Outside, the traffic passed up and down Whitehall and the wind blustered, but this room was soundproof; sound neither came in nor went outside.

"Alec Ryall was a good chap," Merrick said.

Craigie still tapped his thumbnail.

"And he's dead," Merrick went on.

"Quite sure?"

"Badly hurt for certain—and they'd finish him off, anyhow. He'd seen them, could have identified them."

Craigie didn't speak. If his face had been bronzed instead of pale because he was so seldom in the open air, he would have looked for all the world like an image of a Red Indian chief; or a schoolboy's conception of a Sioux, Commanche or deadly Crow. When he puffed out smoke it was as if he were saying: *"How!"* in greeting. But now his eyes showed something besides tiredness, and Merrick, who had worked for

Craigie—which meant for the Secret Service Department called Z—for many years, knew that other look well.

It was pain.

Craigie felt the probable death of Alec Ryall as a man might feel the death of his own son. In some ways he felt it more, because he had sent Ryall to his death—as he had sent other men to theirs. They had known the risk, and he had believed that it was essential to take it; but each time it happened, it hurt.

Merrick knew that.

"And his wife's seen some of them, too." Merrick stood up, tossed his half-smoked cigarette into the fire, and began to walk about the room. "They would want her dead. I hope our boys got to her in time. I wanted to stay—"

"Jim," Craigie said, "you know what happened as well as I do. We had to get that envelope back and fool Vandermin's men with a fake. It was as simple as that."

"Simple?" Merrick spat the word. "It—" he paused, as if fighting down emotion. "All right, simple like Machiavelli. Vandermin—or the abstract thing we call Vandermin, we've never seen him, only heard the name—is now after Gillick and his precious plans. So we watch. Vandermin's men lift the plans. We're quick and Alec gets them back. I'm at hand to pass on the fake. But Alec doesn't get away clean. It all happened near his home, so he tries to put Vandermin's men off the scent but fails. He must be desperate because he involves his wife. And what do *I* do? I make sure that Vandermin can kill her. She's seen his men, and that probably means—"

Merrick broke off.

"If we've fooled Vandermin, it's all been worth while," Craigie said.

Merrick stood in front of him.

"I should damned well hope so," he growled. "If Mrs. Ryall—" he broke off, and forced a grin which didn't touch his eyes, then lit another cigarette. He dropped into the chair again. "Sorry, Gordon. It was seeing Alec, I suppose. Known him a long time. And seeing her, too. She was—terrified. The kind of terror that freezes the blood. Yet she was ready to play. There was a moment when I thought she knew what all this really meant— when I thought she looked at me as much as to say 'If he's dead, I want to die.' Call me crazy!"

He was drawing fiercely at the cigarette.

"She's lovely, isn't she?" Craigie asked gently.

"I—I suppose so."

"Did you tell her Alec was dead?"

"No," Merrick said. "No, I even gave her hope that he was alive, to encourage her to pass off that fake envelope. That was when she seemed to know he was dead." He leaned back and closed his eyes. "Well, she tried—and they probably killed her. I'll grant you one thing—Vandermin thinks that this is big."

"It *is* big," Craigie said quietly, impressively.

Merrick didn't open his eyes, but his voice became sharper; it was as if he were tormented by questions which he knew would never be answered.

"It had better be," he said harshly. "Killing agents isn't important, we know the risk. Killing a woman who doesn't know a thing about it—"

"We had Corlett and others waiting to try to save her," Craigie said. "Why assume the worst?"

Merrick opened his eyes. They were large, blue, frosty. In a way he was good-looking; his features were small and perfectly cut, his mouth was a little too well-shaped. There was hardness or roughness about his features, as if he spent all his time out of doors and was weathered like teak. He was almost like a life-like figure carved from polished wood. But his eyes were expressive, and never more so than now.

"You'll even lie to yourself," Merrick said abruptly, and jumped up again. "You know damned well that there isn't a chance for her. Oh, I don't blame you. I did my allotted share towards killing her, didn't I? And if necessary I'll do it again to-morrow. We have to be tough, don't we?" That was a vicious sneer at himself, at Craigie. "We're the bright boys of British counter-espionage, if we don't behave like the toughest men on earth the old country might get a kick in the pants. Nation first, women and children second. Mind if I have a drink?"

"Help yourself," Craigie said mildly.

Merrick went to the cupboard and opened it. Every shelf was crammed with oddments—shirts, collars, ties, books, tins of food, tobacco, cigarettes, matches—it was like a miniature general store. The whisky and glasses were on the bottom shelf, with a syphon of soda.

"Having one?" Merrick asked abruptly.

"No, thanks."

Merrick poured himself a generous tot, splashed in soda, put everything back and went to his chair. He looked calmer, and there was more colour in his cheeks. He drank half the whisky and soda, then put the glass on the floor by the side of his chair.

"Apologies. Repeat: I suppose it was seeing Judy. She's certainly something to look at. Alec often talked about her—doted on her. His one worry was what would happen to her if he died. I don't mean money, but—emotionally; spiritually. Oh, the hell! He knew how she hated his damned job, although she didn't ask questions. She's like finely tempered steel, he'd often say that—she could bend a long way, but he was afraid she would snap if he died. He—"

24

Merrick stopped and looked at the telephone; it gave a short ring, then a long one. Craigie moved to take it, and Merrick looked as if he were holding his breath.

Craigie said: "No, he's not here . . . Yes, I will." He rang off immediately. "Greenham, for Bill," he said. "Nothing from Barnes yet."

"We ought to have heard by now."

"It won't be much longer."

Merrick tossed the cigarette into the fireplace and lit another, obviously without thinking what he was doing.

"Give it me straight, Gordon. How vital was this step in the job of catching Vandermin? Could we have done it without having Alec killed?"

Craigie didn't answer at once: Merrick didn't prompt him. The one thing Merrick knew was that he would always get the truth from Craigie; there would be no exaggeration, no sugaring of any pill. In the course of twenty-five years, half of the men who had served as Department Z agents had died; or had been maimed for life. Nothing in the long, weary, ceaseless fight against the spies of other nations and of great commercial interests was unknown to Craigie.

At last he said:

"I hoped Alec would get through. I couldn't be sure. We let Vandermin find out that Professor Gillick would be carrying plans of our latest jet aircraft. We let Vandermin steal them from Gillick—then had Alec steal them back, and had the faked ones ready." Craigie spoke slowly and carefully, as if examining each stage for error. "It took careful planning, Jim. There were a dozen places where the scheme could go wrong, and the man most likely to make it work was Alec. But they got after him too quickly. I don't see any other way we could have done it, though. It's vital that Vandermin should think he has the real plans. Because he'll pass them on, and we'll have a chance to find out who's going to get them. We've known that Vandermin was a menace for a long time, but we've never got beyond him. We have to, now. We must find out whether he's an agent for someone else, or a freelance selling on any market that offers. Nothing must stand in the way."

He stopped. There was silence for a few seconds. Then Merrick began to speak, looking as if his fears were less urgent now.

The telephone rang. He stopped speaking and held his breath as Craigie reached for the receiver.

4

NEWS

Y es," Craigie said, and listened, then shot a glance at Merrick, meaning: 'Here's news' . . . "Yes, Roy . . . Oh, fine!" His voice echoed his relief, his delight, and he nodded at Merrick . . . "Look after her . . . Yes, I think so."

He rang off.

Merrick finished his whisky and soda, then walked behind Craigie's chair. He felt a pricking sensation at the back of his eyes, and a tightness in his throat. He had never felt so painfully emotional before. He helped himself to another drink then went back to the fireplace. All this time Craigie talked.

"Corlett and those with him drove the two men away before Mrs. Ryall was killed—then let them escape through a ground-floor window. They've got descriptions—and the taller man ties up with other descriptions we've had of Vandermin, but I can't see him doing this in person. Still, Corlett is following the pair. Mrs. Ryall was unconscious, but a doctor's seen her—she'll be all right. One of our men will stay at the flat for a while—until we decide what to do with her. She was nearly strangled."

Merrick grunted.

"You know," Craigie said gently, "there was once a rule in the Department that no agent should be married. We had to break it, but I often wish we hadn't."

"Can't expect us to be monks," growled Merrick.

Craigie grinned. "No one suggested it! But a married man is under a bigger strain than most. Alec and a dozen others often feel like you felt to-night. It's new to you, and you didn't like it."

Merrick said slowly: "You can't have it both ways—you can't really be married *and* be in this job. Who's after Vandermin's men now?"

"Corlett, as you know—and Bob Kerr."

"Kerr's another married man—with a family! Oh well." Looking much brighter, Merrick sipped his second drink. He didn't speak of Corlett. "Anything else you need me for to-night, or can I go and make a fool of myself with some lovely from London's giddy night life? Even nip across to Paris for a few days? What wouldn't I do for Montparnasse, *les Naturelles*, or even the right bank of the Seine? London is a hell of a dull spot." He was a little too jerky—not quite himself, but much less tense. "Or else, work."

"Stay in London, will you?"

"Yes, sir."

"This job is going to get worse before it's better," Craigie said. "I think it's going to be a long time before we get Vandermin. He's active in the States as well as in South America. We don't want to bring him in until we know all about him—so we have to let him get away with a hell of a lot. We'll need you again, but you can ease off for a bit—Corlett will keep on the job until we find out who these faked plans go to; you may take over from there. By the way, you don't know Elliott, do you?"

"Who is he?"

"One of us—he's been abroad for some time. He's pretty good, and you'll probably be working with him."

"Glad to," Merrick said absently. "Nothing else for now?"

"No, Jim," Craigie said.

"Thanks." Merrick went to the wall and Craigie stretched out a hand to release the door. "I like the new gas chamber where you can give us all the once-over," Merrick said, and grinned a forced grin. "Gordon, any objection to me looking in on Judy Ryall?"

"Not that I can think of."

"Good. Thanks."

"You can tell her the kind of thing that Alec was doing," Craigie said.

There was more wind than ever outside, it was biting cold, and there was a spitting drizzle in the air. Merrick hugged his thick brown coat about him and bent his head as he went towards his car. He couldn't think about anything until he reached it. Then the wind carried the door out of his grip, so viciously he feared that it would be wrenched off. He forced it shut and sat back, hearing the howling wind, seeing people crouching before it, coats billowing, hats flying.

No one watched him.

He started the engine, let in the clutch, and drove off. He wasn't really surprised that he thought of Craigie, not of Judy Ryall; and that once again he marvelled as he left Craigie. It was as if the Department Z chief could read his thoughts; other agents had said the same thing.

Merrick had wanted to tell Judy Ryall what kind of job Alec had always done. The risky, deadly ones. He hadn't been sure that Craigie would agree, hadn't plucked up courage to ask.

He drove off slowly. As some men drove almost automatically, so he looked about and behind him. Over the years a sixth sense had come to him when he was being followed. He wasn't, yet had the uneasy feeling that all was not well. It was like something in his bones. He drove slowly and made several detours. Certainly no one followed him. He lit a cigarette, one-handed, lost control of the car for a moment, and went up on the kerb.

"Steady," he said. "Crazy!"

He drove more steadily until he reached Moor Street, Victoria, and his flat. It was beneath the shadow of the cathedral, surrounded by tall apartment buildings. The street itself was narrow, and there were tall, terraced houses of dark red brick, with steps leading up to each front door. Wind howled down the street and struck the car broadside, almost taking it out of control again. He pulled up outside the house where he had his flat, and waited.

No one appeared.

Three street lamps glowed. Someone passed the end of the street, battling against the wind. Merrick got out, held the door carefully, then slammed it.

It was piercingly cold. He ran for the porch, made it, and took out his key but didn't go in at once. That sixth sense still warned him, and he looked up and down, seeking shadows which might be figures.

No; no one watched.

He went in. There was a narrow passage with a dim light and a flight of stairs immediately in front of him and another light on the landing. His flat was on the top floor; the fourth. It was spacious and he liked it, although there was no lift, which was a nuisance. He whistled softly and still looked about him, peering at corners.

A radio was on in the second flat; Beethoven, noisy. A woman lived there, alone, forty-ish, easy to look at and accommodating. He didn't know her well; he did know that her door had developed a habit of opening when he was coming up or down the stairs; by 'accident'. It didn't open to-night. On the next floor lived a pleasant, elderly couple, the woman with a bad burn scar over her right cheek; no matter how she tried, she couldn't hide it. Merrick had an idea that they were very happy, idyllic. He was on borrowing terms with them—milk, tea, sugar, the little things. Their radio was on, too; Light Programme, Merrick judged.

A lamp burned on at his own landing, everything was quite normal—and yet he had that feeling of being followed. It was probably because of the shock that Judy Ryall had given him. Even now he could hardly believe that it had happened. He had jumped into the room and he had expected a terrified woman, but he hadn't expected terror laid upon a beauty that was unbelievable; indestructible; beauty beyond words.

The funny thing was that he had seen her photograph several times; Alec had shown it to him. It was the same woman all right, yet photographs hadn't done her justice and probably never would.

Thank God she was alive!

He slammed his door, whistled on a high note, and went from room to room deliberately; he looked in all four, including the kitchen. He would have known in a moment if there had been anything wrong. Every room was empty, every window was fastened just as he had left it. Two rattled noisily as the wind struck at them, especially the big kitchen window.

He went into his living-room, which had a sloping ceiling at one side and was very large. There were golf clubs, tennis racquets, other sporting oddments, a small silver cup, horse brasses on a narrow wooden shelf which ran the length of two walls, and pewter tankards between the brasses.

The cream-painted walls could do with another coat. The chairs, of dark hide, had a shabby look; so had the Persian carpet.

Merrick telephoned the Ryalls' flat. A Department Z man answered; Judy was in bed, asleep, well on the way to recovery.

Merrick took out whisky and soda, sat back in an armchair, and told himself that he wouldn't go out again to-night. He wanted to dream. He was astonished at the impression which Alec's wife had made on him. As he drank he realised that there was something else; he was trying to deaden the ache he felt because Alec had been killed. It was one thing to say that he'd known the risk; another to accept the death of a friend philosophically.

In the Department they had been close friends. Too close? Now and again Craigie had hinted at it. Merrick knew that they had been put on different jobs because of it; because sentiment and emotions could disturb a man's judgment, and make him do the wrong thing. That was dangerous and could be deadly. The Department came first. Women and children second—third, fourth, fifth.

He drained his glass.

"What I need is a complete bender," he growled. "I want to go haywire. I want—"

He stopped, lit a cigarette, and forced himself to close his eyes. It would soon be over, and there was the relief of knowing that Judy Ryall was alive. Judy—beauty. Judy. How Alec had talked about her. . . !

Merrick dozed.

He could hear sounds in the background most of the time,

especially that rattling kitchen window. He ought to put wedges in, but it didn't matter. Should he go out, do a night club, find a floosie? Perhaps it would be the thing. Have a good time, find comfort in a woman's arms! He was feeling this too much. He—

Another sound came to his ears. It wasn't loud, but it was different, and much closer than that at the window. He had one of those moments of horror; the kind of moment Judy Ryall must have known. Someone was here. His eyes were closed, and if he opened them wide then whoever it was would see that he was awake. He had to steel himself, to pretend that he was still asleep.

He opened his eyes a fraction.

The window rattled and the rustling sound came again. He began to call himself a fool, but didn't jump up to find out what was causing the unfamiliar noise; he just reached the stage of telling himself that he was letting some quite ordinary thing scare the wits out of him.

Then, through his lashes, he saw a woman's legs.

They were nice legs, shapely, sheathed in nylon. She had nice ankles, too, and neat black shoes of patent leather. That was all he saw, at first. She was about four feet away from him, and as he stared he saw her come a little nearer, a hesitating half-step; as if she were nervous of being seen. He dared to open his eyes wider, so that he could see her mink coat, open; her yellow blouse and black coat and her arms. One was by her side, the other stretched out towards him.

He grunted, stirred, and turned his head so that he could see more. She kept quite still, letting her hand drop to her side. She held nothing—did she? He could see nothing anyhow. On one hand she wore a glove, the other was bare. He settled down again, as if he had turned in his sleep, and soon she moved forward with that hand outstretched.

How had she got in?

What was she going to do?

What should he do? Wait and see? Was her hand empty, or did she carry something so small or fragile that he couldn't see it? If he waited to see what she did, would it be too late to save himself from—what?

He knew that he mustn't take the chance.

She moved again, and now she was within his reach. So he tensed himself, ready to spring. He could take her right wrist, which was stretched out towards him, thrust her away and make sure she could do no harm.

How had she got in?

He hadn't locked or bolted the door, so she might have picked the lock; or someone else could have picked it for her. She might not be alone, someone else might be behind him.

He moved.

It took her completely by surprise. She gave a choking gasp and tried to turn away, but was too late. His fingers closed over her wrist. Something dropped; he heard a tinkling sound as of fragile glass breaking. She pulled at her wrist savagely, but his hold was too tight.

She stopped struggling.

Had there been anyone behind him, Merrick would have been attacked by now; so the girl was alone. He held her at arm's length. She was breathing hard. She wore a tight-fitting little black hat, and the canary yellow blouse beneath the fur coat was tight-fitting too. She was small and nicely built, pretty without being a flawless beauty. He had an odd thought: she looked natural, the type one would pass in Harrods or Fortnum & Mason's or see in the Savoy, and think: 'Hm, nice.' She was well made up, and her lipstick made her face look very pale; perhaps partly through shock.

"Hallo," he said brightly, and let her go. "How did you guess I was lonely?"

She didn't speak.

"Because I am, you know," said Merrick, and beamed at her. He was renowned in the Department for being able to play the fool; and off duty or on Department Z men could be flippant until it made one wince. It was a kind of drug, helping them to face the frequent dangers of their work. "I was just dreaming about someone like you, and thought I would have to go out and get her!" He slid his arm round her waist and squeezed. "Mind coming with me, sweetheart?"

She moved slowly, reluctantly, with his arm round her, and he went into the hall. The door was closed.

"This how you came in? Don't tell me your youth was misspent, too." He pushed the bolt home, kept his arm about her, and went into the bedroom, the little spare room, the kitchen and the bathroom. "And all alone, too," he marvelled. "Wonderful. How did you—"

Quite suddenly she collapsed against him.

5

ANGRY MAN

At first, Merrick thought that the woman was fooling him. He shook her and said lightly:
"Try it the other way, sweetheart, you're heavier than you look." But when he pushed her away, she swayed in the other direction and he had to grab her.

He didn't like the look of her.

He lifted her suddenly. She was very light but her body was stiff. He took her to the long couch, laid her on it, and stood watching closely for several seconds. He still didn't like the look of her. She didn't appear to be breathing. Merrick went down on one knee, and felt for her pulse; there was no sign of movement. Her lips were still, Cupid's bow and slack and—kissable. She was nice, she was pretty, even with that slash of scarlet lipstick. Her clothes were of good quality, everything about her suggested money.

He felt for her heart, beneath her breast; and felt no beating.

He raised her right eyelid. The pupil was so tiny that there hardly seemed to be any. He thought 'so she could have had a shot of morphia before she came', and felt something beneath his surprise; a quiver of fear that she was dead.

He turned her over and started artificial respiration, but had a sense of hopelessness from the beginning. He worked on and on, without result. With sweat dripping from his forehead, and feeling hot and sticky, he gave up. He went to the telephone, stepping cautiously and softly, as if in the presence of death. He took the receiver off and put it to his ear, started to dial, finished, and waited; but heard nothing. He frowned, and looked away from the girl for the first time. He put the receiver back, paused, then lifted it—and there was still no ringing sound; the line was dead.

The line at Ryall's flat had been dead, too.

Merrick dropped his hand to his pocket, for the gun he had carried with him all day. He touched the cold steel, but felt no better for it. That damned kitchen window was rattling wildly. He had to tell Craigie what had happened, but couldn't get through from here.

Was anyone outside?

What would happen if he opened the door?

There was no way of being certain, but he could guess that it wouldn't be healthy.

The girl lay very still.

Merrick moved away from the telephone, and went into the kitchen, closing the door behind him. The window rattled more loudly than any other. He turned the key in the lock, climbed up on to a stool, and opened the window. The wind swept in. He turned back, switched off the light, and climbed out.

He had the agility of a cat; in moments of revelation he would boast that he had once been part of a circus act. Climbing up and down drain pipes and on to roofs was almost as simple for him as walking along the street; almost. There was always a threat of danger.

He looked down at the pitch black area at the back of the house—a small, walled patch of concrete. This backed on to a service alley, then on to a wall belonging to the house opposite.

The only light came from two windows, one immediately opposite him, one almost alongside.

He started to climb down the drain pipe. The wind smashed at him and got beneath his jacket, making it billow out, drawing him away from the wall. He clung on, with no time to think.

Half-way down, he stopped to get his breath back, and to look into the area. He saw nothing. He remembered that feeling that all was not well. He smiled faintly, and started down again. When he dropped on to the concrete, the wind drove him against the wall, making him graze his right hand.

He put it to his lips, and sucked—and the wind dropped. Then he sensed rather than saw someone else; a dark shape against the wall not far off. He stood quite still. The shape was moving towards him. He took his gun from his jacket pocket, covered the shape, and moved towards a gate in the wall; this led to a narrow alley, his one hope of getting to the street from here. He wondered if he could be seen against the pale concrete—whether he had been watched all the time. If he had, surely he would have been stopped by now.

Had the noise of the wind saved him?

He reached the gate.

The shadowy figure was by the same wall, standing still and looking upwards. Only the wind made any sound. Merrick edged along the wall towards the man, drew within a few yards of him, and saw that he was staring upwards.

Merrick did the same, and saw light at his own kitchen

window. So someone had broken in. Then a figure appeared; first a hat, then head and shoulders—and suddenly the hat was whisked away. The man up there grabbed at it, but it sailed upwards and out of sight.

Merrick found himself grinning tensely.

"... *down there!*" the man from the window bellowed.

He'd found the window open, and knew which way Merrick had gone. But the wind carried part of the words away, and the shadowy figure didn't hear. He called:

"What's that?"

"This is it," Merrick whispered, and put the gun away.

Then he launched himself at the man, who didn't know what was happening until Merrick's hands clutched at his throat. That was a mistake, for the collar was turned up against the wind and Merrick couldn't get a grip. The man kicked savagely, but missed. Merrick snatched out the gun, a swift flick of a movement, then smashed at the man's temple with the butt.

Two blows were plenty. His victim sagged back against the wall.

"... he must be there!" bellowed the man from the window; so he couldn't see what was happening in the shadows. "Look out for ... slippery customer!"

"That's right," Merrick said. He turned his back on the man he had knocked out, caught his wrist, then hauled him onto his shoulders in a fireman's hold. He hitched him up, then went unsteadily towards the gate, opened it, and found the alley leading to the street. If the area were watched, probably the street would be.

He didn't ask himself what was happening, just accepted the fact that this was—and that someone wanted to make sure that he couldn't telephone Craigie.

He reached the street.

A man stood by the side of his car; two other cars were drawn up, one in front of his, one on the other side of the road. His only hope was to turn in the opposite direction and reach the corner, but a street lamp glowed there, and with his burden he would almost certainly be seen. There was risk enough without it. He hesitated, still carrying the man, who was a light weight; the weight was no problem. Merrick not only had a prisoner; he was anxious to keep him.

He took a chance.

Carrying the man, he stepped out from the alley and walked several houses along, towards the corner, then turned into a porch. Mounting the steps, he held his breath, expecting to hear a shout. None came. He dumped his burden in a corner.

He knew no one inside the house, but there would be a telephone.

He pressed the bell, then peered along the street. He saw the man by his car move slowly towards him. He drew the gun out again and kept the unsuspecting man covered; there was no need to shoot, the guard turned and walked back.

The door opened.

"Who'ssat?" a block of a man asked gruffly. He stood against a bright light, and his shadow was cast blackly into the street; so was Merrick's. "Who—"

The man, short, squat, almost square, saw the huddled figure in the corner.

"What in heaven's name—" he began.

"Must telephone the police," Merrick whispered. The man by his car would see the light and the shadows and would expect someone to walk out; would be puzzled if they didn't, and would probably come to investigate. "Excuse me." He grabbed his prisoner by the waist and hoisted him over the threshold as the man who had opened the door moved back, bewildered and scared.

Merrick closed the door softly.

"Don't open it again," he said urgently, and let his prisoner go. "Where's the telephone?"

"Why—"

"I must telephone the police. Where is it?"

"In—in there." The man, pointing, was bewildered, but bludgeoned by events into acquiescence. He obviously came from the ground floor flat, for the door of that was ajar. As Merrick moved towards the door, a woman called:

"Who is it, Bert?"

"Sorry," Merrick said, and stepped into the flat. "I want to use your telephone." He smiled at a slim, grey-haired woman. It was the smile which had at once shocked and yet reassured Judy Ryall.

The telephone stood on a table in the narrow hall, and Merrick stepped towards it as the front door bell rang.

"Don't open it!" called Merrick, and snatched up the receiver. For this kind of emergency, 999 would be best; police would be here within minutes, Department Z men had close liaison with the Yard. He dialled. The woman came from a room to stare, and the squat man appeared at the flat door, looking scared. The front door bell rang again.

"Scotland Yard Information Room . . ."

"Miller's man speaking," Merrick said. "Send urgently to Moor 27 Street, Victoria, top flat. Be careful, the men are probably armed."

The man who had answered didn't gasp or show surprise or waste a moment.

"27 Moor Street, Victoria, is that right?"

"Yes. Hurry."

"Yes, sir, I'll send the message at once. You did say Miller, didn't you?"

"Yes," Merrick said. "Thanks." He put the receiver down. The front door bell rang again; it was a night for knocking and ringing. He flashed the reassuring smile at the man and the woman, and went along to the front door, but didn't open it. "Get the hell out of it," he called clearly.

No one answered; but the ringing didn't come again.

There was a pause before he heard a low-pitched voice outside, without being able to distinguish the words. Then footsteps moved away from the house; he heard men running until the sound was muffled by more groaning wind. He showed his relief from the tension by taking out his cigarettes, lighting one, and moving towards the telephone. He wanted to call Craigie now, but there was a risk; before he could identify himself he had to use a cypher, and he didn't want to do that in front of witnesses.

He dialled.

"Could you get some hot water," he asked the woman. "Sorry!" He smiled again. "And have a look at that man, sir— the police will look after him soon." He waited for the woman to disappear and the man to push past him—then heard Craigie's voice.

"K—C—I—double R—" Merrick began to spell his name backwards, a simple system of identification which never failed.

"Yes, Jim," Craigie said.

"I had visitors," Merrick announced very quickly. "I've had to call the police to try to cope at my flat—999. I told them I was a Miller's man. I don't understand it and can't explain now, but I've a prisoner, and you'd better have someone here quickly, to look after him. I'm in a house a few doors from my flat."

"I'll fix it." Craigie's voice was unhurried, but sharper, more incisive. "You all right?"

"More luck than judgment."

"Be careful."

"I'll try," Merrick said, and found himself smiling. He could picture Craigie already dialling a number on one of the other telephones at his desk; or getting up to go to the desk. "Here's something to think about. The decoy—if that's what she was—was a woman, thirty-ish, nice, state of collapse, pin-point pupils—"

Craigie's voice cracked across his.

"Wait, Jim." Craigie went off the line, but Merrick could hear his voice as he spoke into another telephone. The slim grey-haired woman came into the hall with a bowl of water and a towel, the squat man stood close to the prisoner, who was stirring.

Outside, cars roared into the street.

"Hallo, Jim," Craigie said clearly. "Get that woman. Take any chance you like, but get her."

He rang off.

6

DEAD GIRL?

M errick put the receiver down, and moved towards the
door. The bulky figure of the man was by it. The
prisoner began to move, and his eyes flickered. Merrick's lips
were set tightly; he heard cars outside followed by the vicious
roar of a shot. It was carried by the wind, distorted and made
very loud, menacing. Both the man and the woman jumped
violently.

"Bert, what's happening?" cried the woman.

"Keep the doors closed, and be careful with him," Merrick
said. As he reached the door, he used the pistol as a club again;
his prisoner slumped down. The woman screamed. The man
made an ineffectual grab at Merrick, but was scared of
the gun.

Merrick opened the door.

The headlights of a car shone along the street. A man
crouched on the other side of the road, hatless but uniformed;
a car patrol policeman. Another shot came, and its roar
echoed about the street.

Merrick slammed the door and ran down the four steps

into the street. Two police patrol cars were stationary at one
end, with policemen crouching near them, held off by the gun
fire. A private car was moving from outside his house.
Another was drawn up outside that, with its door open. A man
crouched close by this; the police car headlights shone upon
the gun in his hand. He was keeping the police at bay.

"Get under cover!" a policeman across the road yelled at
Merrick, as at a stranger.

It was like a sudden flare-up of action on some half-
forgotten battle-front; all it needed was the rattle of machine-
gun fire or the bursting roar of a hand-grenade. The police
cars were at a standstill, but several police were by them,
creeping forward. They wouldn't be armed; and it took
fantastic courage to go into battle unarmed.

"Take cover!" the man roared.

"It's all right," Merrick called, and the wind carried his
words back to policemen some distance away. He stood
watching the car with the open door—obviously waiting for
passengers. The first of the Vandermin cars was already
drawing out of the street.

"Hurry!" That came from the Vandermin man crouching
by the car outside Merrick's house. He was partly in shadow,
but as he turned his face, Merrick saw him looking towards
the front door of the house, which was open.

Was the unconscious girl still upstairs? Or was she
coming now?

Merrick stood there, gun in hand, with a policeman only a
yard or two behind him. Others on the far side of the road
were getting ready to rush forward. More shots rang out,
loud, terrifying. A policeman fell, another staggered, then all
of them stopped moving. The policeman behind Merrick
muttered something which Merrick didn't catch in the howling, blustering wind.

A man appeared from Merrick's house, carrying the girl over his shoulder.

Merrick grunted, and levelled his gun. He had to get that girl, because Craigie had said so; the risks didn't matter.

He fired at the man's legs.

He saw the man stagger and pitch forward, saw the crouching man by the open car door swing round. Two shots came, with vivid red flashes. A bullet smacked into the wall behind him, another plucked at his shoulder. He fired again, then ran forward. The girl was lying on the pavement, the man who had carried her was leaning against the car with one foot off the ground. He was also groping in his pocket, as if for a gun. The man whom Merrick had shot just slumped down.

Merrick fired again.

The man who had carried the girl snatched his gun out from his pocket and held it high, began to curse and swear.

The police came running, and someone out of Merrick's sight fired at them, but missed. The car suddenly moved off. Its headlights shone on the windows of houses, on lamp-posts and doors, on men standing in doorways. It screeched round the corner as another car came towards it. Merrick moved slowly towards the girl, breathing hard, subconsciously expecting a crash. He heard the squeal of tyres and a grinding noise; then the escaping car moved on. One man was running, now, with the police after him.

Merrick didn't give them a thought.

With a policeman by his side, he went forward, a gun in hand. One wounded man was unconscious with his gun a yard away from him; the other had both hands in sight, and blood streamed from one. The girl lay still where she had been dropped, skirt rucked, lovely legs bent, one shoe hanging on by the toes.

The policeman bent down for the gun.

"Keep still," he said. His voice sounded normal. "Frisk that other chap for a gun, will you?"

"Eh?" Merrick grunted.

"Frisk him for a gun."

"Okay, Harry." More policemen arrived from the other side of the road. The confusion began to sort itself out, and there was no need for Merrick to worry about anyone's gun. He went to the girl, and straightened her limbs. Her head lolled back, her body was curiously stiff. Her face and hands were cold. Her hat had fallen off and her coat was wide open. Merrick lifted her, as a policeman hovered about him.

"She hurt?"

"Shot?"

"I must get her up to my flat," Merrick said, and moved round. His physical strength often startled people, and it surprised the police now. "There's a man three doors along—one of these swine. Hold him, will you? And lead the way up, one of you, another beggar might still be up there."

"Look here, who are—" a policeman began.

"Tell you upstairs," Merrick said, and started towards the open door of his house. Two police went back for his first prisoner.

The fortyish, attractive and probably accommodating neighbour stood half-way down the stairs. She wore a dark green dress which fitted her good figure tightly, and had one hand at her throat. She was handsome in a sharp-featured way, and taller than Merrick.

She came to life.

"Can I—can I help?"

"Hot-water bottles, blankets," Merrick said. "Thanks."

"Doctor—"

"One's coming."

"Oh. All right," she said, and turned and hurried upstairs.

She had long, shapely legs and her tight skirt rode up to her knees. "I won't be long." She ran into her own flat, the door of which was open, while Merrick, followed by two policemen, went on. The nice elderly couple weren't in sight; either the radio had drowned all sounds or they were scared.

Merrick's own door was open; the lock had been picked.

He went in, laid the girl on the couch again, and stood back, studying her, and breathing very hard.

He hadn't expected to win the round, but he'd won, and there was cause for satisfaction; deep cause. A job like this didn't crop up more than once or twice a year, if that; circumstances had forced some of Vandermin's men into a corner, and how they'd fought!

He wished the doctor would come.

The girl's face was still very pale; undoubtedly she looked dead. Why had Craigie been so anxious to capture her? What was it all about? One fact was clear—vital things were happening or Vandermin would not have risked a street battle.

Soon there would be more police, the Press, and more Department Z men . . .

Merrick took out cigarettes and turned to the two policemen. One was a sergeant; neither of them wore a hat, and their hair was blown about by the wind, turning them into uniformed golliwogs. They seemed awed, but the sergeant overcame that.

"No, thanks," he said, to a cigarette. "Who *are* you?"

"Sorry," Merrick said. He lit a cigarette and fumbled in his inside pocket, then drew out a card. It showed him to be a Special Branch man, and was signed by the Assistant Commissioner at Scotland Yard and by the Home Secretary. There was a water-marked Z and other fancy tricks in the card to prevent forgery; but these men weren't thinking of forgery.

"Oh, I see!"

"Good job, you fellows did," Merrick said.

"*We* did? Why, you just walked into trouble!" the sergeant touched Merrick's shoulder, where a bullet had cut the cloth. Merrick shrugged and turned away, drawing at the cigarette.

"My boss will be here soon," he said. He reached the whisky and soda, by the side of his chair. "Have a spot?"

"No, thanks. Who is the woman?"

"I wish I knew. Nice looking, isn't she?" Merrick poured himself out a drink, then heard footsteps, looked up and saw the tall neighbour hurrying in, with blankets over her arms, two hot-water bottles in her hands. She clicked her tongue impatiently when she saw that the men hadn't brought blankets from this bedroom, and took possession. She placed the hot-water bottles, wrapped the mink coat more tightly round the girl and covered her with blankets. She tucked the girl's feet in; so it looked almost as if a mummy were lying on the couch; only the pale face showed.

"You're sure a doctor's coming?"

"Quite sure."

"She looks—dreadful."

"That's right."

The neighbour looked at him curiously. She had fine green eyes; bold eyes. In fact all her features were bold, and so was her manner; that and the fact that she was inches taller than Merrick probably accounted for the fact that they were only acquaintances.

"Drink?" he asked. "Gin and something?"

"Well—"

Men were coming upstairs. Merrick poured out a gin and Italian, and was handing it to the neighbour when the men appeared. There were three. One was big and ungainly looking, with greying dark hair, untidy, and one heavy lock falling over his forehead. He was curiously ugly; homely was perhaps the better word, with a plump face, heavy features and a forehead lined with a scowl. Behind him came a tall, thin man, testy-looking and carrying a black case.

He walked straight to the girl.

The neighbour joined him.

The third newcomer was another police-sergeant, who came to check the disconnected telephone.

The big man moved towards Merrick, a little unsteadily; he sat on the arm of Merrick's chair, and grinned. That made all the difference in the world to his expression; in a flash he became handsome.

His name was Loftus, and he was Craigie's second-in-command. He limped because he had an artificial leg, acquired, as he liked to say, in the Department's service.

"Nice work, Jim. Very nice."

"Yes, isn't she?"

Loftus grinned. "We've been looking for the lovely for a long time. Tell you all about it, soon." He lowered his voice. "Cataleptic."

"Cata—" began Merrick, and stopped, marvelling.

"She seems to be able to go into a fit at will," said Loftus. "We want to find out why she does it. As soon as we can we'll get her away from here, to the Home for the Aged and Infirm." He grinned again. "Tired?"

"Not by a long way."

"That's good," Loftus said, "because you've hardly started yet. Let's have the story."

Merrick talked . . .

The doctor examined the girl, then she was taken downstairs by ambulance men. Merrick went on talking. Department Z men came in, two of them research chemists he knew only slightly.

"The girl had a glass phial or something in her hand, and

Merrick thinks it broke," said Loftus. "Have a look round, will you? Where did that glass fall, Jim?"

Merrick moved to the spot where the girl had been when he had startled her.

The light glinted on splinters of glass.

The chemists started work at once, going down on their knees, using torches, then opening bottles, turning the room into a laboratory. Merrick knew enough to ask no questions.

The police-sergeant said that the telephone was working again; a cable on the landing had been cut.

"Did you take a peek at the lovely's handbag?" Loftus asked.

Merrick grinned. "I left it to the boss!"

"You mean you forgot it," Loftus said, and shrugged. They moved towards a small table, where the girl's handbag lay. "Ten to one there's nothing in it." He shook out the contents; powder compact, lipstick, two keys, a purse, a red handker-chief, a white lace handkerchief, a small wallet, a golden cross. Loftus picked up the wallet. In it were several letters, and one photograph. It was more than a snapshot—the face of a remarkably good-looking man, obviously cut down from a head and shoulders portrait.

Loftus said gently: "And that makes me wrong. A name, Iris Arden. An address—King's Court, Fulham. And a boy friend. The chap who ran away from Judy Ryall's flat was a handsome type, I'm told. Corlett wouldn't get that wrong, would he?"

Merrick said: "No."

"Let's get this address covered," Loftus said.

He went to the telephone.

It was rather like pressing a series of buttons and knowing that each would get things on the move. He arranged for men to go to the address in Fulham; for others to find out if the handsome man was known there; for copies of the photograph to be made; and for the man who was

51

watching Judy Ryall's assailant to meet them at Craigie's office.

It took ten minutes.

The chemists were still busy.

"It's too bad," one said, with a knife in his hand, "but you're going to need a new carpet, Jim. We want this bit."

Merrick kept a blank face.

"Help yourself to anything," he said blandly. "Have a good time."

He and Loftus went out.

He didn't ask questions . . .

They drove in Loftus's car to Whitehall, and went through the rigmarole of getting in. Craigie was alone, and this time at his desk, writing. He finished what he was doing before looking up. Then:

"Hallo, Jim, you've been busy. Thanks."

"Pleasure."

"It might help a lot," Craigie said, "although we've tackled all the prisoners and none of them has talked. They may soften up later, we'll have to see what we can do." He pulled at his meerschaum. "Iris Arden's under observation at the Home—how much have you told Jim, Bill?"

"Nothing," Loftus said.

"Hm." Craigie stood up. He was of middle height, although very spare; he looked short. "Jim, everything we told you earlier still holds, with a plus we didn't mention. Two or three times our chaps have got very close to Vandermin, or Vandermin's men. Each time they've just blacked out. Two were found, looking as if they were dead, but they recovered. The only things common to each were these: each talked to a girl answering Iris Arden's description; each felt a scratch on his hand; each lost consciousness soon afterwards, and each seemed to be dead. It was like a form of catalepsy, but without any of the usual signs of animation. Understand?" He was almost abrupt.

"I'm beginning to," Merrick said slowly.

"We've our research men busy on it, and it may not be too serious, but the stuff has the effect of knock-out drops. We can't be sure, but it seems as quick as curare, a matter of minutes from scratch to unconsciousness. Iris Arden's the first one we've been able to get and put under observation—that's why she mattered so much. It looks as if a phial broke in her hands and she scratched herself with the stuff. We'll find out."

"And she was to black me out."

"It looks like it," Craigie said.

"And don't ask us why," Loftus murmured.

Merrick said: "No, chum. She picked the lock while I was out and waited for me in the loft, I expect. I sensed that something was wrong. I—"

He broke off, for a buzzer sounded, and a green light showed on the mantelpiece. Craigie pressed a button on the desk and Loftus went across to the door in the wall which had a glass label on it on this side.

"Okay," he said. "It's Corlett."

Merrick sensed that both Loftus and Craigie looked at him sharply, but neither spoke again. He didn't speak either, but felt himself go tense. It was a pity, but Corlett, one of the Department's best agents, was a man he didn't like. The dislike was mutual. It was difficult to explain, as if they were allergic to each other. They had worked together once or twice but were kept apart as often as they could be. This case looked like bringing them together.

The door slid open and Corlett came in.

Obviously he expected to see Merrick, and he nodded and smiled. That smile was half the trouble, for Merrick was never sure when it was meant to be a sneer. Corlett was in the thir-

ties, tall, lean, sleek, handsome, with jet black hair and magnificent eyes—a legacy from his Spanish mother. There was
something almost feline about him; and almost feminine too;
yet his courage was legendary, almost as renowned as Alec
Ryall's.

"Hallo, everyone," he said. "Quite a night. Why did I have to
leave my sacred post?"

"I wanted you to see this," Craigie said, and picked up the
photograph of the handsome man which had been taken from
Iris Arden's bag. "Do you know him?"

Corlett studied it for a moment; and smiled. It was a
sardonic smile, and managed to suggest that Craigie really
shouldn't worry him with such obvious trifles as this.

"Oh, yes."

"Who is he?"

"The man who was at Ryall's flat to-night, with the other
type, called Kip," Corlett said. "Judy Ryall told us that this man
called himself Malcolm Wright. But I'd come across him
earlier, and he was then known as Arden, with an address in
Chelsea, and a pretty wife."

"King's Court?" asked Craigie.

Corlett nodded.

"So Malcolm Wright is also Arden, and the woman Iris is
probably his wife," Craigie said. "She was wearing a wedding-
ring." He pulled at his meerschaum. "Thanks, Roy. Keep on to
him, won't you?"

"Leech-like," promised Corlett. "At the moment he and Kip
are in a house at Hampstead, as I told you. I hope they're still at
home when I get back." There was an implied reproof again—
that he shouldn't have been called here. "Nothing else?"

"Not yet," Craigie said.

Corlett went off.

Neither Craigie nor Loftus spoke of him when he had

gone; Merrick wondered if he were right in thinking that they also disliked the man. If they did, would they use him?

Craigie said: "You'd better get back and get some sleep, Jim. We're through for to-night. Judy Ryall's at the Home, and safe enough while she's there. As she's seen Arden, *alias* Wright, she'll probably be in danger the moment she comes out. Your job is to watch her."

Merrick's eyes glinted.

"I had a feeling that you wouldn't object," Craigie said dryly.

7
BRIGHT MORNING

Merrick whistled as he bathed, whistled most of the time that he shaved, hummed as he prepared a breakfast hearty enough for a condemned man—while in his dressing-gown—and hummed and whistled while he was dressing.

The sun shone.

It was half-past nine, and he had slept well. The one job in the world that he wanted was to look after Judy Ryall, and he had the job. Understanding fella, Gordon Craigie. As soon as Judy came out of the Home for the Aged and Infirm, Merrick's duties would start. That satisfied him, and he was not easily satisfied.

Craigie had promised to telephone him; but the bell was silent.

Merrick went to the living-room, and looked into the street. Nothing indicated the violent scene of the night before, but then, violence was like that—a swift surge, deadliness, followed by a fading away into memory, as something unreal and half-remembered.

He knew that one of the prisoners had died—he, Merrick,

had killed him. The one with the wounded leg and hand wasn't seriously hurt. He didn't know whether Iris Arden had come out of her 'cataleptic fit'. There was a lot he didn't know.

Only Craigie and Loftus, and perhaps one or two special agents, ever saw the whole picture. He, Merrick, and a hundred other Department Z men saw parts of it. It was as if they were looking for one piece of a puzzle, and, having found it, handed it over to Loftus or Craigie for them to see where it fitted. There were times when it was extremely unsatisfactory, because one wanted to see everything. But years of service had taught him that it didn't greatly matter. He would have a job to do, and do it, and forget it until the next job came along.

He hoped he wouldn't have to see too much of Corlett.

He had known himself with nothing to do for Craigie for three months; and also known times when he had been working at pressure for six months at a stretch. That had been a strain. It *was* a strain; as when he had been told to get Iris, and had walked out to get her.

He'd had the breaks again.

He knew much more about this particular affair than he had known about any others. Craigie had been unusually frank. There was Vandermin, known by name and reputation as a spy, known to have access to a lot of secret information, known to run a highly efficient organization; and Craigie wanted to find out everything he could about Vandermin and his principles, while Vandermin fought back.

Merrick whistled. The cheerfulness wasn't wholly real; it was a front, a kind of protective device. He would not let himself dwell on the probability of Alec Ryall's death. The Department toughened one; no agent dared give way to his emotions, but had to beat them back. That flippancy helped. The next best thing to being heartless was to sound heartless. One could almost fool oneself.

The telephone bell rang.

"That'll be Craigie," he said aloud, and hurried from the window to the instrument, dropped into his chair and swung his legs over the arm. "Jim Merrick speaking."

"Good morning, Mr. Merrick," a man said.

The voice was unfamiliar; that of a stranger. There was a curious ring about it, a hint of sarcasm, which Merrick picked up very quickly.

"Morning," he said briskly.

"My name is Arden," the man said. "I think you know my wife."

There wasn't much time to think; but thoughts flashed through Merrick's mind. Did Arden know that he was being watched? What was the line to take? Aggression? Timidity? He fell back on Department flippancy.

"Why, hallo," he said brightly. "I could hardly believe my ears—how *are* you? Delighted to hear from you again. There isn't a man I'd rather put in the lock-up. Your wife wasn't well, and—"

"I want to know where she is," Arden said, "and I want her back. You'll help to arrange it."

"Oh," said Merrick, as if startled. His voice went shrill. "Really? Why don't you come and talk about it? I'll have half Scotland Yard and a few military around, to put down the scarlet carpet. You know the address, don't you?"

"If you want to see Alec Ryall again, you won't set any trap. I'm coming to see you," Arden said, and rang off.

Merrick put the receiver down slowly.

He had been frowning when he had talked flippantly, and was frowning now. He dialled Craigie's number, but Loftus answered; Craigie was 'out' which probably meant in some other part of the building.

Merrick reported . . .

"If he comes, see him," said Loftus. "Don't lay anything on. Let him think you'll listen to his terms."

"Right. What about Corlett? Is he still watching Arden?"

"Yes. He'll be around."

"I see," Merrick said. "Another thing, Bill. I think Alec's dead. Shall I pretend I think he's alive?"

"Do anything that might make Arden talk," Loftus said. "Try to find out what's on his mind. Is he scared? Is he prepared to take risks to get his Iris back? Or is he trying to fool us?"

"Right."

Loftus went on: "Another thing, Jim, I could name someone who feels sure that Alec's alive."

After a pause, Merrick said: "Judy?"

"Yes."

"How is she?"

"Much better. Stiff neck and all that, but more herself. She's a remarkable woman."

"I'll talk to Arden, then," Merrick said abruptly, "but Corlett will have him followed, there'll be no need for me to chase after him."

"None at all."

"Thanks," Merrick said.

He broke off, and lit another cigarette. The sun was shining outside, and a woman opened a window and shook a duster out of it and the sun shone brightly on her fair hair, making it glisten. Merrick saw but hardly noticed her. She disappeared, leaving the window open. There was no wind at all, the gale had blown itself out.

Merrick finished the cigarette, started another, and then stubbed it irritably.

"Damned sight too much smoking," he said aloud, and went to the window and stood looking into the street. A milk van was there; a greengrocer's cart was drawn up near a corner, and two housewives and a maid were gathered about it. Two dogs, one smooth-haired terrier and a mongrel that was mostly Irish setter, frisked along the kerb.

Merrick kept his thoughts moving.

Why had Iris Arden come to see him? What had she meant to do? What would Arden say? What would justify him taking the risk of coming and declaring in advance that he was on his way?

A small car turned into the street.

It pulled up outside the house, and Merrick pressed close against the window to catch a glimpse of the man who climbed out. It was a large man, rather big round the middle, dressed in a dark grey suit, and with a small but very white bald patch in the middle of sleek dark hair. He didn't look up, but moved quickly towards the street door—which was open by day. He carried a brief-case under his left arm, and moved briskly.

Soon, the flat's front door bell rang.

Merrick went to open it.

Arden was handsome, but a bigger man than Merrick had expected. He was fleshy, big round the middle, and immaculately dressed. His trousers had knife-pleated creases. He had a close clipped grey moustache and a high colour. His eyes were small and very dark brown—wary eyes, which moved all the time. His mouth was unexpectedly small and the lips very red.

They sized each other up.

"Come in," Merrick said.

"Thank you." Arden stepped past him, then waited for Merrick to close the door and lead the way into the living-room. It wasn't much after ten o'clock. "Sit down," Merrick said, and watched the other man closely.

"Prefer to stand," Arden said. "I want my wife."

"I can understand it."

"Where is she?"

"Don't be silly," Merrick said.

"I'm quite serious. Unless she is returned to me, unhurt, you'll never see Alec Ryall again."

Merrick said very slowly: "How do I know that he's alive?"

"Oh, he's alive," Arden said almost brusquely. "He was badly hurt, but we have first-class doctors and surgeons at our disposal. It will be some time before he can move about again freely and I doubt whether he will be any use to you people in future, but he's alive."

He made it sound convincing; but it might be a studied plausibility, put across because he was anxious for Merrick—and Craigie, for that matter—to believe that Alec Ryall wasn't dead.

"Where is Iris?" Arden demanded abruptly.

"Well cared for."

"Merrick, you don't seem to understand. Ryall can easily be allowed to die."

"Oh," said Merrick, and forced himself to grin. "Charming way to put it. Not that he can be murdered, bumped off, killed, choked or croaked, but sweetly allowed to die." He beamed. "Cheerful thought, and death certificate provided, all arrangements made with discretion, sympathy and decorum. I'm talking about the funeral, of course. Come off it, Arden."

"If you want Ryall back, you can have him, in return for my wife." Arden almost barked the words.

"Thanks. Does Vandermin approve of this?"

Arden didn't answer. He looked slightly ruffled, as might a City man who had just lost a few thousands on what had seemed a sound investment; or whose advice on the market hadn't been taken. The amazing thing was his apparent confidence.

"And she'd better not be hurt," he said in a hectoring voice.

"Oh, rather not," agreed Merrick earnestly. "All goods exchanged in best condition, no blemishes, bruises, cut throats or broken vertebrae guaranteed. How's Kip?"

"I neither understand nor like your manner," Arden said loftily, and turned towards the door. "I understand that you are a close friend of Alec Ryall's."

"Do you?"

"Does this organization that you serve make you so utterly cold-blooded?" demanded Arden, huffily. He turned towards the door. "I shall telephone later in the day to make arrangements. Will you be in at three o'clock this afternoon?"

"Can be," murmured Merrick.

"Be good enough to be here," said Arden.

He was unbelievable.

Merrick watched him go out, walking stiffly, with the brief-case hitched under his arm. All he needed to make the picture complete was a black Homburg and an umbrella. He went briskly downstairs, and Merrick watched him out of sight. No one appeared to follow; but Corlett was good, Arden was being followed all right.

Merrick went to telephone Loftus or Craigie.

Craigie was still out.

Merrick reported . . .

"Much more in it than meets the eyes," Loftus said. "We'll have to work it out. Oh—go and see Judy Ryall, will you? We've told her to expect you."

8

'FOR THE AGED AND INFIRM'

The members of Department Z boasted a kind of vernacular all their own. It was based upon their use of facetiousness and flippancy as a relief from tension and anti-dote to danger. The tensions which took possession of them could have carried them to screaming pitch, could have tossed them over the line between sanity and madness, but for this relief. It was cultivated by practically every member of the Department; a few, who were never in tune, were simply the exceptions and usually short-lived. Challenged on the subject, Merrick and many others would probably give a one-sided grin, and say:

"We have to find a laugh somewhere, chaps. How about spending a night in the Home?"

It would not, by ordinary standards, be funny; but it would amuse them, or at least occupy their minds and take their thoughts off the grimness, the dourness and the deadliness of their work.

The Home for the Aged and Infirm was a case in point.

It was, in fact, a nursing home which was run by Department Z agents as doctors, nurses, all the staff. Only injured or sick agents and prisoners, such as Iris Arden, went there. The police knew what it was; the police also knew that many strange things went on there. If it were vital to get information from a prisoner, then Craigie and Loftus would stop at nothing to get it.

Since for the most part Department Z was a young man's organization and since the people who engaged it in a form of battle were usually young, old folk were seldom at the Home. The staff was youthful, also; and so, with that heavy, somewhat laboured and occasionally irritating wit, it had become the Home for the Aged and Infirm.

There Merrick would stay, if he were hurt.

He did not park his car too near the Home, but in a side street some distance away. The nearest main road was Park Lane. Merrick walked briskly, without an overcoat and hatless, through a calmness which seemed to have no relation to the boisterous storm of the night before. The sun shone gently and it was warm, and the trees were beginning to burst their buds. Now and again he caught glimpses of Hyde Park, which looked superb with its early spring grass, a vivid green after the winter rains. He was not interested in Hyde Park, but in whether he was followed.

He was.

A tallish, youthful-looking man with a slightly vacant air, carrying a furled umbrella and wearing a narrow peaked cap, all very new, had driven behind him in an M.G. two-seater; and was now walking after him. Merrick did not go to the Home, but turned a corner, and waited for the stranger.

The stranger appeared.

They stood and weighed each other up, and on the stranger's somewhat vacant if good-looking face there appeared a soothing smile. He had a generous moustache of chestnut brown colour, like his hair. He was not as young as he looked.

"No villain, I," he said in a deep voice. "The name is Elliott. Double T, so to speak, O, I, double L and a final E. Mind if I see that no one cuts off your tail?"

Merrick grinned.

"No one warned me we'd been among the fashion-plates."

"Dear fellow," protested Elliott, "no offence taken. I understand you're on the way to the Home for the Aged. Sympathies. If it helps you to feel less decrepit, be vitriolic by all means. Should we stand and chatter quite like this?"

"Supposing we go different ways."

"Oh, no," breathed Elliott. "My orders are orders, and they are not to let you out of my sight from this day forth. I've just taken over a bed-sitter on the second floor of the house opposite yours in Moor Street, by the way, and that tall and handsome Mrs. Gilmour will be our undoing unless you're careful. Lead on, Jim Merrick."

Merrick grinned, and turned.

Elliott was fifty yards behind him when he went into Ambrose Square. Several houses had been destroyed by the bombing and one was left with gaps on either side. This was the Home. Remarkable things happened at the square. Workmen were always in possession of some main or other; or building walls or taking walls down or digging holes or filling holes up; and failing that, there were painters or pointers. In fact the Home was kept under close surveillance, by night and day; but no attempt had ever been made to invade its sanctuary.

To-day, two men were earnestly contemplating a gas main hole.

Merrick went into the Home, which had a brass plate inscribed:

THE AMBROSE NURSING HOME

and was greeted by a fresh-faced, dark-haired and blue-eyed woman in starched cap and apron.

"Hallo, Mr. Merrick, nice to see you again—you want to visit Mrs. Ryall, don't you?"

"Thanks. How is she?"

"Oh, she'll be all right, if—" the Sister-in-Charge paused, "—if we could cheer her up a bit. She's so worried about her husband. Worried isn't quite the word, but you know what I mean."

"Obsessional," Merrick said. "Yes. Mind if I use your telephone?"

"Of course not. You know where my room is, don't you? I'm just going up to see the other woman patient—she's come round and pretends she doesn't know what happened." The Sister hurried upstairs on a pair of sturdy legs, and Merrick went into her tidy office, dialled the office in Whitehall, and when Craigie answered, said:

"Merrick here," and went through the formula. Then: "Is a thirty-fivish, country tweeds type with a woof-woof voice, named Elliott, the one of us I was warned about?"

Craigie chuckled. "Yes."

"Then he wants to learn how to tail without being spotted in ten seconds dead."

"He's been your shadow for a week," Craigie said, mildly.

"He—" began Merrick, and bit on his words. "Then where the hell was he last night?"

"Watching," Craigie said. "You didn't need his help after all, so the other side still don't know what he's like to look at."

Merrick said: "Oh." He gave himself a moment to digest that, then asked: "What do you make of Arden's visit?"

"I don't know yet."

"Wish I did," said Merrick. "He'd know that we'd follow him, guess what he was asking for. Why should he ask? I don't get it." He paused. "But if you don't either, why should I feel shame? Any last-minute instructions?"

"Help Judy all you can."

"Hum," said Merrick.

"There is something more," Craigie said. "Iris Arden swears she doesn't remember anything that happened last night. Look in on her, and see if you can make her admit that she recognises you. Lay everything on with Sister Alice."

"Right," said Merrick.

He walked slowly up the stairs, and heard Sister Alice's voice, giving instructions to a nurse. Then the Sister rustled out of a room, and stopped short at sight of Merrick.

"What's the matter, Mr. Merrick?"

"Work to do. Will Iris Arden recognise me?"

"Oh," said Sister. "Well, she's in Ward 9, and if you go in, I'll watch through the window and judge her expression. Are you going straight in?"

"Please."

They turned, and Sister Alice went into Ward 8—which was usually kept empty, because it had one of those windows which could be seen through in one direction, but seemed like frosted glass in the other. Her starched dress rustled. Merrick stopped at the other door for a moment, then turned the handle slowly.

His thoughts flashed back to the night before, when he had been dozing, and when this girl had approached him with outstretched hand.

He opened the door slowly.

She was sitting up in bed, sideways to the door, looking at a magazine. She wore a fluffy blue bed-jacket, her hair was nicely done—fair hair, with ringlets—and she was made up. She looked healthy and well; bonny was the word which sprang to Merrick's mind. He saw how her long lashes curled and swept her cheek.

He stepped inside; and she didn't notice him.

He didn't close the door, but took a step forward, one hand outstretched, the other by his side; just as she had on the previous night. He took another step; a third; and then she realised that there was someone present.

She turned her head swiftly, terror leapt into her blue eyes, her mouth dropped open.

"You!" she breathed.

"That's right, sweetheart," said Merrick. "Nice to know you remember me." He grinned and went forward, sat on the edge of the bed, and looked into her eyes. The terror was receding but she was still frightened. "Why did you come to see me last night?"

"I—I didn't! I've never seen—"

"You're a bit late with that one," Merrick said. "Why did you come? How long had you been in the attic? What were you going to do?"

She looked at him mutely.

He said: "My pretty, take advice from me and tell the truth before you get hurt. This isn't a game for sweet young things. People get shot, killed, wounded and all twisted up." He wasn't smiling now, but leaning forward and uttering the words softly; trying hard to frighten her—and knowing that as soon as he had left, other agents would come in and try to break her down. "Why did you come, what were you going to do?"

She shrank back on her pillows.

"I ought to break your neck," he growled. "Do you know a man named Kip?"

"I—"

"Do you?"

"I—yes, yes, he works for my husband!"

"And Vandermin—do you know Vandermin?"

"No!" she cried. "No!"

"That's a lie."

"It isn't, it's true!"

"You know Vandermin!"

"I don't know, I swear I don't." She tried to get further away from him.

He wondered why she was so frightened; even wondered if in fact she was. Her eyes looked huge. He thought that she was probably neurotic; perhaps the basic catalepsy cause was some nervous strain. She was pretty, although all her colour had gone.

"Sweetheart," he said softly. "I can see that you're going to get hurt before long."

He got up abruptly, and went out. Sister Alice met him outside. She was a member of the Department, although only on the fringe of most events. She was troubled by some of the methods it was necessary to use; to her, patients were just patients.

She looked troubled now.

"She isn't well, you know," she said.

"Tell Craigie just what happened, will you?" Merrick asked. "Sorry."

Sister Alice nodded and turned away. Merrick shrugged, and went along to the next floor, up a wide staircase. An elderly man was polishing the wooden floor; what part had he played in the Department's life, Merrick wondered. He suddenly saw himself, in twenty years' time, polishing floors. He grinned—but the grin faded as he stopped outside Judy's door.

His heart beat a little faster.

Since he had leapt into that room at Barnes and seen her, the picture of her beauty had been in his mind's eye nearly all the time. It went deep. He had a sickening, guilty feeling about it. She was Alec's wife, and even if Alec were dead, he was newly dead. There was doubt, now—or reason for doubt—whether he had been killed. All Merrick knew for certain was that this woman, wife of his closest friend in the Department, had seemed to possess something vital, something which could rip all pretence away, could sweep the ground from under his feet.

That had happened.

He tapped, and heard a husky voice, saying: "Come in." He opened the door and went in, smiling as he had smiled when he had seen her the previous night. Like Iris Arden, she was sitting up in bed; her fluffy bed-jacket was pink. She was small—not tiny, just small—and of her beauty there could not be a moment's doubt.

Her eyes were huge, blue, glorious.

She wore a bandage round her neck, but that was the only sign of injury.

She recognised him at once. The look of inquiry faded from her eyes. She dropped the book she was reading. Her cheeks had been faintly pink, but the colour ebbed from them.

He closed the door.

"Hallo," he said. "I'm glad you're better."

He went across to her, smiling, knowing that she was already reassured, wondering if she would ever know how his heart thumped. Nothing like this had ever happened to him before—and subconsciously he had realised that from the moment he had set eyes on her; now, he knew beyond all doubt. She mattered. She was part of the weft and weave of his life; he was as sure of that as he was sure that he was walking towards her.

"I thought—I wouldn't see you again," she said huskily.

"Oh, I always turn up when least expected." He pulled up a chair and sat down. "Nice job you did last night. Thanks."

She didn't speak, just watched him.

"The little show is nearly over," Merrick went on. "You know it is what the romantics call the Secret Service, I imagine." He smiled, as if that were a mild little joke.

"Yes." Her voice was very husky, because of the bruising, but clear enough.

"All you have to do is stay here until everything's died down, and then—"

"No," she said abruptly. Her voice was more strained, and she probably tried to shout. "No, I can't stay here." The words came so readily that he knew she had been turning them over and over in her mind; obsession was a word he had already used about her. "No, I must find Alec."

"We're trying," Merrick said reassuringly. "We hope—"

"Please," she said, and moved a hand as if to restrain him physically from going on. "I know you think—I know that everyone thinks he's dead. I'm sure he isn't. There's something that tells me—"

She broke off.

Merrick said: "If he's alive, we'll find him, Judy. And he'd be hard to kill." He tried to force a smile. He knew that the words were ludicrous, almost grotesque; he knew that it would for ever be difficult to speak sensibly to her. He could tell that she had this obsession; she could believe in 'something that tells me' that Alec was alive. Reason played no part in that.

And he was detailed to protect her!

For the first time, he doubted the wisdom of that; wondered if for once Craigie had made a mistake.

"He *is* alive," Judy said tensely.

"Of course he is," said a man who pushed the door wide

open and stepped briskly in. "Sit still, Merrick! Don't move, Mrs. Ryall."

He spoke as if he were in complete authority.

It was Arden.

9

THE RAID

Arden looked exactly as he had when Merrick had last seen him, even to the brown brief-case under his arm. He seemed annoyed, or testy—rather like the doctor the previous night. He moved forward very lightly, like many big men. Behind him was a smaller man whom Merrick hadn't seen before.

Judy screamed.

Merrick stood up, slowly. His gun was still in his pocket, and he was between both men and the bed. He could hardly absorb what had happened—that they had been able to force their way in. It was almost as if they could walk through brick walls.

"Don't take your gun out," Arden said, "you'll only get hurt." He looked at Judy, while she stared in terror at the second man.

This one was small, with hatchet-thin features and a long nose; he was grinning, and it wasn't a pleasant thing to see. He had two teeth missing from the side of his upper jaw; and the gap showed. He had long arms and very big, knobbly hands; and he held a revolver.

This would be 'Kip'.

Merrick's hand was still out of his pocket; he knew that the second man could shoot him before he could fire. He had one trick up his sleeve; his acrobatic ability to move from a standing start.

He was ready to leap.

"We don't mean any harm to you or Mrs. Ryall," Arden said. "We've come for my wife." He shot Merrick a haughty glance. "I made you think I was going to parley with you. Consequently neither you nor your friends expected me to raid this place so soon, did you?"

There was nothing to say.

"I knew quite well that I was being followed," Arden went on, superciliously. "As I was already known by your agents, I could do no harm by visiting you. It is fairly easy to guess your reactions, Merrick, and those of your colleagues. I was fully persuaded that you would let me go."

Merrick still didn't speak.

Outside, there were the gas-men; watching. Inside were several Department Z men on a spell of duty. Arden couldn't get away with this, but could hardly know it.

Couldn't he get away?

He had forced his way in.

Judy, rigid with fear, stared at the smaller man. She seemed to be able to look only at his hands—the hands that had nearly strangled her.

Only seconds passed, before someone downstairs screamed. The sound was cut off, very short; but it had come.

Kip's big mouth grinned more widely, the gap showed up more.

"I want you to understand this, Mrs. Ryall," said Arden

earnestly. "Your husband is alive—injured but not danger-ously. He will be all right." That matter-of-factness carried its own conviction; and the words and the tone of the voice made Judy look away from Kip. "He will remain so, Mrs. Ryall, while you remain sensible. Don't work with Merrick or any of these people. Whatever they ask you to do, refuse. Understand? It is very important because it might affect your husband's safety. He'll be all right, provided you do nothing to help them. Remember that."

"Ye—yes," Judy muttered.

Merrick knew that this was phony. Arden was trying to reassure them, that was all; was playing cat-and-mouse. Merrick tried to convince himself that it was right to be patient; to wait. He could jump at the men, but—what was happening outside? Had Arden brought others with him?

Arden flicked his right thumb.

Something shimmered in the light, just in front of Merrick's eyes; and burst against his lips. He wasn't sure what it was. He smelt the sudden overpowering stench of ammonia, which burned his nose, his eyes, his mouth—a searing breath of it went down his throat.

Blind, pain-racked, he leapt forward, with no idea what he was doing; panic-stricken. Something brushed against him. Then the door slammed.

He was alive . . .

The burning at his mouth, nose and eyes seemed to get worse, the pain in his chest was greater than he could bear; and there was worse; the fear that Judy was suffering, too. He didn't know where she was, didn't know whether he was near the window or the door. And he could hardly breathe, it was as if his windpipe and his lungs were shrivelling up.

Then he began to black out.

He knew that he was falling, and tried to turn his shoulder

to the floor; but he smashed his head against the wooden flooring, and more pain went through him. He was unconscious a split second later.

A dozen men in gas masks moved through the Home for the Age and Infirm, briskly, business-like. They went through ward after ward. Patients and nurses were lying on their chairs, on their pillows, asleep; gassed. Sister Alice was in her office, slumped across her desk, breathing softly. The old man who had been polishing the floor was sitting against a wall, his chin on his chest; looking more dead than alive.

Everyone except the raiders slept.

Arden, Kip and others checked room after room, and eventually found the prisoner who had been shot in the hand and the leg, on a ground floor ward. He was bandaged and dozing. They carried him out to a waiting ambulance.

They went into the Square in twos, with Arden bringing up the rear. He was very brisk. He looked up and down the Square, importantly. The two gasmen were no longer in sight; they were actually inside the hole they had been digging; planks of wood had been placed above it, by the raiders, hiding them. A private car stood at one corner, and Arden, Kip and another man hurried towards it.

"I hope we don't have to have more gunplay," said Arden. "I always dislike it and I'm quite sure that it does more harm than good." He spoke exactly as he had to Merrick.

They reached the car, and climbed in; before the doors closed the driver, who had the engine running, started off. The ambulance was also on the move, with the rest of the men inside.

No one followed them.

Arden leaned back in his seat, and said: "Ah, well, that's over. A very neat job, I think we can all agree. Very satisfactory. What fools they are to think that they can defeat us!"

He chuckled, a high-pitched, rather silly little chuckle. Kip laughed, huskily. The other man and the driver didn't join in.

The car and the ambulance moved into Park Lane, then into the Park itself, then towards Knightsbridge. No one followed them.

The lean Elliott, with his country-looking tweeds and narrow cap and plaintive voice, watched from the window of a house opposite, as Arden and his men left the Home. Elliott had a telephone in his hand, and from time to time made cryptic remarks into the mouthpiece. He sat in an easy chair with his legs up on a stool; the curtain hid him from anyone in the street.

One was taking off a gas mask, as Elliott said . . .

". . . Got the car description and number? . . . Good man, William . . . The Arden chappie is now coming out, with the Kip cove . . . three others are carrying a bandaged hero, probably the chap we collared last night . . . You got the description of the ambulance, didn't you? . . . I say, old chap, I hope we don't slip up on this. The police radio cars are following these wallahs, aren't they?"

"Yes," said Loftus grimly.

"Well, that seems about the lot," said Elliott. "Half a sec, though . . . Arden is hurrying along to the big Austin at the end of the street, square, beg pardon, with Kip. Amazing what long arms Kip has . . . In they get and off they go . . . Can I go and pick up pieces across the road now?"

"You wait for ten minutes," Loftus said. "More of our fellows will soon be at the square, and they'll have a spare gas mask. We aren't taking more chances."

"That's it," said Elliott, enthusiastically, "be thorough in all things, I'd hate to be gassed. Er—we won't lose 'em, Bill, will we? I mean, Roy Corlett must have slipped up, and—"

"He and his men were laid out," Loftus said grimly. "Vandermin's men attacked everywhere at once—but we had a double watch, and Arden will be followed all right."

"Well, I hope so," said Elliott. "I'll possess my soul in patience, meanwhile."

"Quite sure they didn't bring Judy Ryall out?"

"Oh, yes, old chap. Which doesn't mean they didn't kill her, does it?" Elliott asked.

Ten minutes later a Rolls-Bentley turned into Ambrose Square and pulled up outside the Home. A few people moved about the Square, having no reason to suspect trouble. Elliott hurried across and joined the men from the Rolls-Bentley. Corlett, sleek and self-possessed, with a bruise on his temple, was one of them. Elliott judged from their faces that they didn't look forward to what they might find.

"At the ready," Elliott said, brightly. "I'm going in to have a sniff first. There shouldn't be any gas about in the halls and whatnot, but there might be in one or two rooms."

"Go and be the hero," Corlett said. It was the kind of remark which ruffled Merrick.

"Oh, but I will," said Elliott earnestly.

They sniffed at the open front door; sniffed in the hall; came to the conclusion that the gas had not lingered. All of the doors of the wards had been left open. Some of the nurses were already stirring. They found no sign of any trouble until they reached the closed door of Judy Ryall's room.

"Steady here," Elliott said.

"As you say, sir," Corlett murmured.

Elliott opened the door a fraction of an inch, and sniffed. Gas caught his breath and made his throat burn, brought tears to his eyes. He slammed the door. Corlett and two others slipped on gas masks and went in, leaving Elliott in the passage.

Corlett paused.

Merrick was stretched out on the floor, his face mottled, his eyes closed, his mouth slack. Judy Ryall was in bed, lying on her back, looking just the same as Merrick. One Department Z man leapt across the room and thrust the window up; another pushed the bed towards the window; a third went out and ran down the stairs, to telephone.

The two resident doctors were coming round from the gas.

Corlett called the Whitehall office and talked to a doctor at the same time.

10
DISAPPEARANCES

Loftus sat at one of the big desks in the office: Craigie at another. Bob Kerr, a tall, heavily built man, was with them—the only one who was inactive. Loftus had one telephone, Craigie a second; and the receiver was off a third. Each man was making notes, and talking against each other in a low-pitched voice; there was a continual muttering in the room.

"Kensington High Street," Loftus said. "Yes . . . that's the ambulance . . . Car nearing Hammersmith Broadway . . . I'll hold on."

"Yes, I've sent Billitter round," Craigie said. "He's the best man we have on respiratory troubles, undoubtedly the right man for Merrick . . . Sure they're both alive? . . . Well, that's something . . . Tell Elliott to go home and take it easy until I need him again . . . good."

Craigie rang off.

Loftus said: "Ambulance heading for Hammersmith, too . . . Hammersmith people alerted, I hope . . . Good."

Craigie picked up the receiver which had been off its cradle. He spoke in a voice as calm and unflustered as if this were an inquiry about the weather.

"Hallo, Mark . . . Yes, the man I'm interested in is Joshua Arden; he seems important . . . I don't know, yet, possibly something in the City . . . We were hoping to get something from his wife but he's spirited her away . . . Yes, if you'll dig up all you can about them, that'll be fine, especially overseas contacts . . . Yes, all seems to be going pretty well, we're tracing them thanks to your people . . . they're heading west. As soon as I know any more, I'll tell you. Thanks."

He rang off again.

Loftus was saying: "Arden's car's just turned on to the Great West Road at Brentford, the ambulance is near Turnham Green . . . Yes, noted, I'll hold on."

He glanced at Kerr and looked across at Craigie.

"Should be all right, but we can't be so sure when they're in the country. I've got two cars after them, picked them up at Hammersmith, and I've instructed the drivers not to let Arden know that he's being followed. I could change that by radio."

"No. Let him think he's fooled us," Craigie decided.

"That's all right—provided he hasn't," Loftus growled. One-handed, he lit a cigarette, while Craigie got up, to walk about the room. "I'd no idea they knew about the Home. They're good. Almost as if—"

He stopped, but Craigie didn't speak.

Loftus drew deeply at the cigarette.

"We've known about Vandermin for a long time, but we didn't know enough," Craigie said at last. "He's much bigger than we thought." He didn't sound so much agitated as worried. "And the disturbing thing is that he's obviously too familiar with us. He knew the Home, and knew that his wife—

81

if she is his wife—had been taken there. He was able to deal with the men working on the gas mains, and we can take it that he has pretty accurate knowledge about how we watch the Home—and probably other things."

Loftus said: "Yes. And what else does he know about?"

Craigie didn't speak. Kerr lit a cigarette, and watched the other two.

Now that they had relaxed for a few minutes, although Loftus still had the telephone, reaction set in. They saw—or admitted—the significance of what had happened for the first time. There had been danger from someone known as Vandermin, and sure knowledge that he was an extraordinary spy who could call on powerful assistance; then suddenly it had been discovered that he had been spying on the Department.

"We could call Herrington in," Loftus said.

Craigie shook his head slowly. "No."

There was a buzz, followed by a green light. Kerr got up at once and went to the sliding door.

"Corlett," he announced.

"Let him in," Craigie said.

Kerr pressed the switch, and Corlett stepped in, fingering his bruised head. He reported, briefly, and Craigie made little comment. The tension in the room was painful to each one.

"Hallo," Loftus said into the telephone. "Yes . . . car at the end of the Great West Road near Staines, ambulance half-way along it, going in the same direction. Good, thanks. Yes, I'll hold on for a bit longer." He leaned back, then stubbed out his cigarette. "I wish I didn't feel there was a chance that they would show us a clean pair of heels, Gordon. So we don't bring Herrington in?"

"Not yet. He might be the essential cog the whole thing will turn on before it's over. We'll have him concentrate on Arden now." Craigie smoothed down his thin grey hair with both hands. He looked more tired than ever; and there was something else in his expression; anxiety, even a kind of shock. "I wonder why Herrington didn't tell us about Arden before."

"Who is Herrington?" Corlett asked, and gave his superior smile. "An agent we haven't the privilege of knowing?"

Craigie said flatly: "Yes, Roy, a card up our sleeve."

Loftus said: "Well, we can't . . . Hallo," he called into the telephone. *"What?"* He stood up slowly, and his expression was so startled, so incredulous, that Craigie leaned across the desk and grabbed an extension; Corlett did the same, and they heard the caller say:

"Our two cars following the ambulance were crashed on the Great West Road. A police car waiting for them near Staines reservoir was also smashed." The man was speaking quickly, excitedly. "There's no trace of the ambulance or the car we were after . . ."

"Get a radio message out, with the description of the car and the ambulance. Do everything." Loftus nearly howled the order.

"We will," the man said. "Don't worry."

He rang off.

Corlett put down his receiver slowly.

"Not good, are we?" he said sardonically. "You need fresh blood, Gordon. I let the gentry put me out, and all of our brilliant agents are being led up the garden. You couldn't be letting Vandermin fool himself into thinking that he has us on the run, could you?"

Loftus sat back in his chair, and Craigie squatted on the corner of the desk, without saying a word.

"It's almost as if they're playing with us, and we're on the spot," Loftus said thinly.

Two hours later they were told that the ambulance had

been found in the river, south of Staines; and the car which Arden had escaped in was found in a quarry not far away. There was no trace of fingerprints, nothing to help.

Jim Merrick came round slowly.

At first, he did not remember what had happened. He knew only that he was comfortable but very thirsty, and that there was a slight pain in his chest. It did not worry him a great deal. He dozed off again, and came round several times with the same feeling of lethargy, the same lack of all desire to think. The pain was always nagging at his chest. The last time he came round, his thirst was such that it tormented him, and he could not drop off. He opened his eyes and tried to speak, but heard a hoarse sound which wasn't at all like his voice; even making it hurt his throat.

But someone heard.

A nurse was there, round-faced, smiling; just a head and face and a white cap and a smile. But she gave him something out of a spoon, which soaked into his parched tongue and the roof of his mouth, and couldn't have been cooler. He lapped it up, and sank back, feeling much better; so much better that he was able to drop off to sleep again.

That happened several times.

The moment came when he woke, in daylight, and remembered a little of what had happened; chiefly the horror which had come when the gas had bitten at his mouth and nose and eyes, and seared his windpipe; he could understand why his chest hurt, now. He didn't call out this time, but managed to raise his head and look about him. This was a small room, or ward; and no one was there. That surprised and in a way annoyed him, but there was nothing he could do about it. He dropped back on to his pillow, but didn't fall asleep again, and he heard footsteps. He was looking up when the door opened and a nurse and a young doctor looked in. Merrick thought 'doctor' because of the long white coat and the stethoscope hanging round his long neck.

They looked surprised to see Merrick awake.

That was the moment when Merrick thought of Judy. Memory stabbed at him. She had been in the room with him, might have suffered as much as he. He croaked her name, but only made a harsh, unrecognisable sound.

The nurse spooned the nectar into his mouth.

"Judy—Judy Ryall," he muttered, when he had finished swallowing.

They understood at last, and the doctor gave a quick, reassuring smile; he was a nice-looking young man with a snub nose.

"Oh, she's going along nicely. Much better than you, but we'll soon have you right."

"Sure—sure she is?"

"Quite sure."

"Oh," said Merrick weakly. "Good." He felt himself smiling, because he wanted to smile at the knowledge that Judy was all right; he was actually worse than she. He dozed off again. When he came round, the first thing he remembered was Judy, but there was no fear in him, because he also remembered that she was not in danger.

He wanted to see her.

He did not see her for three days. It was not until afterwards that he knew that until the end of the third day, he was considered to be still on the danger list. The gas had done a lot of damage to the membranes of the chest and throat. It was going to be months before he was really himself again. Judy was much better, he knew, but she would also need a spell of convalescence.

On the fourth day, she was wheeled in to see him, smiled, was cheerful, seemed reassured with life. She wasn't allowed to stay long. The picture of her beauty, with that mass of lovely, burnished hair and those huge blue eyes, stayed with Merrick for a long time.

After that she was wheeled in most days.

Then Merrick was allowed to get up. He discovered then that he had been unconscious for a week, while doctors had despaired of his life. So it was nearly three weeks from the time of the raid on the Home to the moment when he first stood on his own feet again; although 'stood' was a euphemism. He staggered, and would have collapsed but for a watchful and expectant nurse and doctor.

The worst thing was the difficulty with breathing. It no longer hurt, as it had done, but any movement made him gasp for breath—gasp as if he couldn't breathe at all. Judy had the same trouble.

Merrick wanted to know what had happened to Arden and the others, but although Craigie came once and Loftus several times, neither of them went into any detail. The implication of their silence was obvious; Arden had escaped.

Corlett hadn't been a conspicuous success . . . and they weren't making any progress.

To win ground, Alec had taken desperate risks.

Merrick found himself almost two people at the same time. There was the longing to see Judy, the desperate anxiety to talk to her, the almost obsessional hope that she would begin to feel the same about him. And then, in moments of revulsion against himself, there was bitterness at the fact that Alec had died for nothing. It had been a complete waste of a life.

He was in such a mood when Loftus came to see him.

"I know, Jim," Loftus said, after Merrick had talked for ten minutes, savagely. "I've often felt the same. But just now we're scared. Vandermin knows a lot more about us than we know about him. He follows our chaps about. He knows our hide-outs, habits, tricks. We've never been up against anything quite like this."

Loftus wouldn't say that unless it were literally true.

"Understand that, Jim—we are the counter-espionage unit of the country, and we're being outwitted. Think what that means."

Merrick didn't speak; but thought . . .

"Arden just put a finger to his nose at us and vanished," Loftus went on. "We've got to find him, and Alec Ryall might still be able to help us."

Merrick didn't speak.

"He might still be alive," Loftus said.

Merrick began hotly: "Damn it, you can't think he's betraying—" and then broke off, hardly able to breathe.

Loftus handed him a nasal spray, which helped; after a few minutes, Merrick breathed more normally.

"Bill," he said, "if this is how it's going to be with me for the rest of my days, I'd rather—"

"You'll get completely well," Loftus assured him, and brushed the heavy lock of hair off his forehead. "No doubt at all. Both you and Judy will. Listen, Jim, we must discover whether Alec is alive or dead. It wasn't until he disappeared that we had any evidence that Vandermin had this confidential information about us. Alec was a senior agent, and knew a great deal. It's possible that he's a prisoner, and they've found a way to make him talk."

The possibility was so obvious that it hurt.

"We have to find out whether he's giving this stuff away or whether Vandermin's getting it from somewhere else," said Loftus. "And something's happened to give us half a chance. They're still interested in Judy Ryall. She's watched at the

Home, and, whenever she goes for a walk or a car ride. They could have killed her, but didn't. If Alec's alive and they want to keep him talking, they might try to kidnap Judy—and threaten to torture her if he won't talk freely. It's a possibility anyway. We're making sure that she can't be kidnapped—yet. But if she were working for us, they could kidnap her—and she could fool them."

Merrick didn't speak.

"She would know what to look for and how to get a message back to us. We'd have a real chance," Loftus said. "You're both going to Switzerland for convalescence, and you'll be away for two or three months. In that time, we want you to get Judy to work for us, brief her, make sure that she'll do everything she can."

Loftus stopped.

Merrick said harshly: "Isn't it enough to murder Alec? Must you kill her too? Must you kill—"

He couldn't go on, his breath was so short. He almost choked until Loftus pumped the spray in front of his nose. This time it took longer to recover. He knew that he mustn't exert himself; it hurt too much. He mustn't get excited. But he had to make a decision. He had to decide whether to try to persuade Judy to sacrifice herself.

He could argue as much as he liked, could even question the logic of it. If they wanted her, why hadn't they taken her from the Home? That kind of question kept coming to mind, and Loftus's only answer must be that they'd decided to kidnap her after that raid. The probable motive was plain enough.

"Listen, Jim," Loftus said. "We're not playing for a set of plans or a formula, we're playing for the security of the whole Department. There was never a job that mattered so much. Even if Alec did die for it . . ."

He went on and on; with overwhelming arguments.

"All right," Merrick said at last, and tried not to shout or wave his arms about. "All right, I'll try. But if anything happens to her, I'll—"

"Take it easy," Loftus said. "Take it easy."

Merrick sat there, gasping for breath.

11

LETTERS

M errick walked briskly along the wooden veranda of the chalet, looking over the distant, snow-capped mountains. Below were fertile valleys, green from the snows of winter, not far away the sleek-skinned cows ambled, their bells ringing so that when the snows came again they could be found easily and taken down to the security of the valleys.

Just within sight was the small wooden hut which housed this end of the cable car railway which led from a narrow mountain road, itself leading from the St. Gotthard Pass. The sun glinted on the single cable, and shone, bright and ever-moving, on the stream which ran down the mountainside near this line, dancing and leaping over rocks, looking for all the world as if it were gambolling and could never become the deadly, menacing torrent which, when the snows melted, it became every year.

Merrick reached the steps leading to the grounds, and ran down them. He had never felt fitter. It was easy to forget that he had known what it was to be breathless after the slightest exertion. He was smiling and bronzed; looked more than ever like a model carved out of teak. Moreover, he smiled freely and easily, and there was a look of contentment in his grey eyes.

Judy was walking towards him from the cable car.

She walked quickly, too, although she was coming uphill. The sun was behind Merrick and shining on her, and it gave her an almost unearthly beauty. As he drew nearer, he had to stop to watch. It was not only beauty of face and figure but of movement; easy flowing, confident movement. She wore a woollen jumper of bright green, and a black, flared skirt, black walking shoes, nylons. As she drew nearer, she tossed back her hair, and the wind ruffled the smooth waves and the sun gleamed upon them. Her eyes were huge; and there was happiness in them, although Merrick knew how quickly that happiness could fade, in memory.

They met.

They gripped hands; because Merrick took hers. He made himself let her go.

"Hallo! Had a good time?"

"Mm-mm."

"Much shopping?"

"Oddments," Judy said, "just a few souvenirs, Jim."

"Some for me?"

"Certainly not!"

He made a mock grimace.

"I shall blame you, woman." They had turned and were walking towards the chalet together. Now its roof hid the sun, and they did not have to narrow their eyes. The wooden building was large, with a veranda facing east and west, the windows were uncurtained. By night, beds were moved to the verandas for those patients who still needed to sleep in the open air but it was essentially for convalescents, and was never used for bad or chronic cases.

They went up the steps.

Judy had been to the village, and it had taken her since early morning. A Department man had followed her. Merrick had made a pretext to stay behind, because he did not want her to feel that she could not move without him. Inwardly, he had hated the fact that she had been willing, almost eager, to go on her own. There were moments when he was sure that she cared no more for him than she did for one of the nurses; for the doctor; for any helpful friend. At other times, he dared to hope that she might one day . . .

He was utterly, helplessly, in love.

The lilt of her voice, the movement of her head or of her body, had beauty for him. All day he had tried to think of the things he would soon have to say to her; and all day he had been haunted by pictures of her.

It was now the beginning of July. Down in the valleys it was hot; but here it was always cool, even though on day after day the sun shone out of a cloudless sky, and glistened as diamonds on the frozen snow within sight; melting a tiny fraction on the surface so that water dripped ceaselessly down the sides of the roads.

There was one good thing; most of the time, Judy was completely natural. Alec Ryall's fear that if he died she would break up, hadn't been justified; in a way, Alec had thought he mattered to her more than he had.

Was that really true?

At heart, Merrick knew that it wasn't. The truth was simply that she did not believe that Alec was dead. In a way, she lived for the day when they would meet again. She hadn't talked about it often; but once, last week, she had been able to discuss it without her voice breaking, without tears flooding her eyes. So she was now in complete command of herself.

They went into the small lounge, which was exclusively

theirs; it overlooked the north and the west, and the sun flooded a corner of the room, with its cream-painted walls, its light brown parquet flooring, Persian rugs and wooden furniture. There were no other patients here, but three servants—all in Department service.

Judy dropped her bag on a couch.

"Collect any post?" asked Merrick. Post had to be brought up from the bottom of the cable.

"Two for you, one for me," Judy said. "I haven't looked at mine yet." She tossed back her head again, and raised her arms, putting her hands beneath her hair and lifting it. If she knew what a figure she made, how Merrick's heart pounded, she would never do that. "Isn't the view lovely?"

Merrick said: "Never seen a better."

Something in his voice made her look at him. She dropped her hands. In moments like that, he realised that probably she did know what he felt—or was it possible that she didn't really think deeply enough about him?

She didn't look away.

Merrick did.

The maid came in to ask in her attractive broken English whether they would like some tea. Merrick forced heartiness into his voice, and in a few seconds things were outwardly normal again. Judy spread her purchases out on a table—two cow-bells, a wooden carving of a chalet interior, other carvings—and Merrick had his letters. He recognised Elliott's handwriting; Elliott was the one agent who had kept in touch with him—much as Alec would have done. The other was type-written, with a London postmark. So was Judy's, he could see that.

She wasn't very interested in her letter, probably because she guessed who it was from, and it wasn't important.

"Pretty things," Merrick agreed, lightly. "Now I'm going to see whether I've been sentenced."

"Sentenced?"

"To return to England. I can't stay here for ever, more's the pity." He grimaced. "I've work to do."

She had been smiling, but the smile faded. Every time he referred to 'work' the same thing happened. That was the one thing they had discussed; his work, Alec's, the general principle of what they had been doing. He had discovered that she was fiercely loyal; oddly, she hadn't once complained of the need for sacrifice, although the hurt was still raw.

"I suppose so," she said, "I'll be back in a few minutes, Jim."

She went out; he wondered what emotion had driven her away. Her letter was still on the table, resting against the cowbells. He picked it up. It had been typed on a different machine from his letter. He opened Elliott's, which said very little, was just a lively report on trifling incidents; somehow like Elliott, with his big moustache and his woof-woof voice and his casualness.

The other was from Loftus—brief, almost brusque:

"Dear Jim,

"The time has come, as the walrus said, to try to get cracking. Tackle Judy at once, will you? And cable me what she says.

"Be very careful; we know that the chalet is being watched. Our boys are handy, of course, but you know what I mean.

"Glad to know you're feeling yourself again. Gordon adds regards.

"As ever,"

So it had come.

He had now to try to persuade Judy to work for the Department; to take the risks which Alec had taken. Loftus hadn't gone into detail and the letter was almost formal;

certainly it was emphatic. There was plenty to indicate that Vandermin was active again.

From correspondence with Loftus and Craigie, Merrick knew that things had been quiet.

But the chalet was watched . . .

Merrick looked out of the window. There were other chalets within sight; he knew the occupants of some of them, who liked it up here in the winter; others were complete strangers. He had often been conscious of that feeling of being watched—it was hardly necessary for Loftus to make sure that he was careful.

The months there had given Merrick plenty of time for reflection; he had been able to convince himself that the Department not only did but should come first. He had felt something of the alarm that Loftus and Craigie felt about Vandermin's knowledge of the Department's secrets. He was like Alec, like every agent; once he had served for a few years, he was a slave to the Department.

He saw the sun glint on something, a long way off. He moved his position. High above them, on a spur of rock with snow behind it, a man with binoculars was looking this way. Merrick hadn't seen him before, and couldn't imagine what he was looking at—except this chalet.

It added to the feeling of uneasiness; as Loftus's letter had done.

This idyll was nearly over.

The sooner he talked to Judy the better.

She came in, quite calm, looking serene; not smiling, but so very natural. The maid brought in the tea almost immediately afterwards. Judy poured out. Watching her slim, tanned hand and arm, Merrick found himself gritting his teeth. She meant so much, and the intimacy they had known here had seemed a permanent reality; but it wasn't going to last. He must get the emotional bee out of his bonnet.

She handed him a cup of tea.

"Thanks," he said, and caught her eye, then looked out of the window. The sun glinted on those glasses. It might be that which made him more on edge, less in command of his own feeling. "I—Judy—"

She said: "Jim, don't please."

He put his cup down; she sipped her tea. She knew what was in his mind, and she also fought against it—in a way, was afraid of it. He knew that now.

"All right," he said, and forced himself to be calm. "I won't be difficult. But before we leave here there's one thing I just have to say. It would be true if Alec were here with us. I love you so much that—"

"Jim," she said, and there was a catch in her breath. "Don't let's talk about it, don't let's spoil things. You've been—so good."

Merrick said: "The good Judy. And—so very right."

He didn't move towards her again.

Loftus's words and Loftus's face intruded. Here was the moment to tell her how she might be able to find out; but too much crowded his mind and there was no quiet in him.

"Let's—let's have tea," she said, as if desperately. "It'll be cold." Her voice had a brittleness which wasn't often there.

They hardly said a word.

For something to do, she picked up her letter and opened it. Because she was looking at it, and not at him, he was able to watch her. At first, her features were composed but had a sense of strain. Next moment all that vanished, her colour fled, her eyes took on a great light, and she jumped up and cried:

"It's from Alec!"

12

SUGGESTION

The light in Judy's eyes was hurtful; blinding. She stared at Merrick as if a new world had opened before her, and then she turned her eyes back to the letter and read greedily, hungrily. It was the moment which told him what little chance he had, and strangely, it did not distress him; it was as if he had emptied all the emotion out of himself, and could be unemotional and dispassionate again.

It wasn't a long letter.

She dropped it to her lap.

"He's all right," she said in a whisper. "He's been ill but he's all right. He—"

She didn't finish, but handed Merrick the letter. He took it, reluctantly. He had no desire to read a love letter from Alec to her, yet obviously she was anxious that he should read it for himself.

"My darling,

I haven't been able to write before. I was in a bad way, I'm told, but am better now. On special work. When this job is over I think we'll be able to settle down to a normal existence. Don't worry. I'm a kind of prisoner, but in no danger.

There *may* be a chance to meet, my darling. I can't be sure—but be ready for a message. I'll try to tell you where to meet me. *But*—don't tell others.

I *will* manage it somehow.

All my love,

Alec."

It might be Alec's writing, too; it looked like it, hurried and rather careless, uneven, schoolboyish. Merrick wasn't really sure.

"Positive it's his writing?" Merrick asked quietly. "Look closely, Judy. Don't—"

"I'd recognise it anywhere!" But she wanted to believe that Alec was alive, so she would be easily convinced. Expert opinion was needed soon; urgently.

He handed the letter back.

"I knew it," Judy said, as if exalted. "I was quite sure. Did you know?"

"No. What special work?"

"You must be convinced now, though," Judy said, as if something in his expression suggested that he wasn't really sure. "Aren't you?"

Merrick said: "Judy, I'll believe that Alec's alive when I see him. God knows I hope he is! This squares up with some of the things that have happened—he says he's a kind of prisoner. The people we were working against certainly took him away from the flat, I saw them from the roof of the house. I wish I knew what he meant by 'a kind of' and I wish I knew why he had written to you." But he knew; Arden wanted Judy, would prefer it if she left Merrick and walked out on the Department. Wasn't that likely? Or was the letter like Arden's visit—

suggesting that they had plenty of time while actually danger was close.

He could still keep calm; dispassionate.

"He'd want me to know he was all right," Judy said.

"Obvious, yes." Merrick forced a smile; it cost him a big effort, but came with fair semblance of naturalness. "What I mean is, if he's a prisoner, why did his captors choose this moment to allow him to write and reassure you?" He picked up the envelope. "London postmark, three days ago." He paused; then: "All right, Judy, let's assume that Alec's alive. I can tell you one thing—his real employers, my chiefs, have thought so for a long time."

She didn't speak; but her eyes asked: "Why didn't you tell me?" and burned with reproach.

He went on, almost harshly: "Alec was a senior agent. Senior to me and most others. Not many knew more than he. From the time he disappeared, the people we've been fighting showed that they had certain confidential information—the kind of stuff Alec could have given them. They're clever devils. My chiefs thought that probably they had found a way of persuading Alec to tell what he knew."

Judy said: "Oh, *no!*"

"Now listen to me," growled Merrick, "our job's a deadly one. You know that by now. It isn't any use shutting your eyes to possibilities. It could have happened. The tone of this letter— if it's genuine—suggests that it is. 'A kind of prisoner.'" He couldn't look into Judy's eyes, something in their expression stopped him. "I'd give anything in the world to make sure whether he is."

After a long pause, she said:

"You mean, if he's a traitor." Her voice was full of disbelief.

"Methods of persuasion—"

"I think I see why you don't really believe in the letter,"

Judy said. This was a moment when he knew that she had much greater qualities than Alec had ever realised; a steeliness; a capacity for dispassionate thought; the courage needed to rise above her emotions. "If the letter is genuine, he's bright and cheerful, a 'kind of prisoner', almost a willing prisoner, selling what he knows for his life." She paused, and her eyes demanded the truth: "Is that what you would read into the letter, if it were really his?"

"I suppose so," Merrick said slowly.

"And your leaders have thought that for some time?"

"They've thought that the other people might be getting information out of Alec," Merrick admitted.

Judy said: "Jim, you knew him as well as anyone. I'd never met you, but often heard about you. I've never told you that before. I know Alec had a tremendous regard for you and great respect, as well as—as liking. Do you seriously think he could be a traitor?"

"I'd want absolute, irrefutable proof," Merrick said.

"Thank you for saying that," Judy smiled gently, gratefully. "I should, too. I just don't believe that it's possible. But if he's not, then that letter—"

She broke off, fighting back emotion. It was her battle, he could do nothing to help her. He gave her a cigarette, and lit up. She looked out of the window, towards the unseen man who was watching them; and then back at Merrick.

"I must find out, somehow," she said with a tense note in her voice. "Is there a way?"

"I don't—know."

"There must be!"

Merrick said: "My big shots are as anxious to find out as you are, for a different reason. Try to see it this way, Judy." He began to walk about the room. "This is counter-espionage. The people who killed or kidnapped Alec have had a long run.

They're getting secret information and they're learning different things about us—our codes, cyphers, habits, agents, methods, hide-outs. It is absolutely vital that we should find out where they're getting the information from. Is it Alec? If we can be sure it is, there's no need to look elsewhere, no need to fear that there are traitors in the Department. But if Alec's dead, then someone else must be giving it away. Does that make sense?"

"Yes," she said very quietly. "I can see all that. Can your chiefs suggest a way of finding out?"

"They've made a suggestion. When they first put it up to me I hated the idea. But the job gets into your blood eventually; you put it first, above everything and everyone else. It dehumanises you," he added; and that was how he felt.

Judy stuck to the point.

"What did they suggest?"

Merrick answered quickly, quietly:

"That you should find out whether he's alive."

"Don't be silly," Judy said, and for a moment her face almost cleared.

Merrick had to chuckle at the tone of her voice; and the moment was refreshing; it took much of the strain out of the atmosphere, and the last vestige of the emotional crisis vanished. They were back where they were, good and close friends.

"I know what you mean," he said. "But it isn't quite so idiotic as it seems. The other people, call them the enemy, tried to kill you twice. Since then, they've shown a lot of interest in you. We've been watched, even here." He saw her start. "We don't understand why they're still interested, but we think—"

He paused.

"I believe I can see what you mean," said Judy, in a far-off voice. "You think that Alec has insisted that I'm not to be hurt—or he would refuse to help."

"Yes," Merrick said abruptly. "That's it." He stubbed out his cigarette, and lit another. "There's something else. We think they'll probably try to kidnap you, so that you can go to Alec. He knows how completely—utterly—devoted you are. And he's desperately in love with you. It's possible that he realises that he'll never be able to come back to ordinary life because he knows the truth will be discovered. But his friends could kidnap you, and take you to him; or with that letter, persuade you to go and join him. You'd be together then, but working on a different side. That's why we think they're watching you."

Judy didn't speak.

"Judy," said Merrick with difficulty, "we don't know that they'll try to get you away, but it's more than a guess. It would fit the circumstances, is an obvious possibility. So—"

"Will I let myself be kidnapped," Judy said in that far-off voice, "so as to find out the truth?"

"That's it," Merrick said. She had seen everything clearly and gone straight to the heart of the matter. Now he had no doubt about her quality; and, watching her expression, her quiet beauty, none about her courage.

"What you want is for me to be kidnapped, and to find out if Alec's alive and if he's giving this information away," Judy said calmly. "Also to find a way of telling you. Isn't that it? You want me to spy on Alec?"

Merrick growled: "I suppose that's the way you'd see it."

"Surely it's the way it is."

He didn't answer.

"I can see how anxious you and your leaders must be to find out where the leakage comes from," said Judy, "but I trust Alec, you know. I simply don't believe that he would do this." She looked at the letter, and Merrick guessed what was going through her mind. If the letter were genuine, then Alec was probably hand-in-glove with spies, was a traitor. So, the letter was false.

Judy stood up. The letter fell to the floor.

"Supposing I say yes? Supposing I agree to try to help? How can I send you a message?"

Merrick was ready for that.

"You'll be briefed. You'll give a sign meaning yes, a different one for no. Details don't matter now, but—"

He hated the job more than ever.

"What else is there, Jim?" Judy asked, in a softer voice. "What worries you so much?"

"The danger to you," Merrick said abruptly. "Face it, Judy. This thing could be deadly. You might be able to tell us what's happening, but if they found out that you were spying on them they wouldn't have any mercy. Alec might be alive, but—" he stopped, stood in front of her and took her hands and held them tightly. "The leader of the Department has what he calls a little black book. It's a book of names of agents who have been killed—not who are just missing, but are known to have been killed. The total is over one hundred and thirty. It's a dirty, deadly, vicious business, and I don't want you—"

She *smiled*.

He was so startled that he let her hands fall. The smile wasn't gay, wasn't callous, but came slowly, gently, oddly reassuring.

"*I* mustn't soil my hands! Alec can, you can, a hundred and thirty men can die for the sake of this Department, but *I* must be sitting somewhere safe and sound, away from all the contamination and the danger. Jim," she went on, taking his hands in turn and squeezing. "You're really something, aren't you? But honestly—I don't know whether I can do it. And I don't know simply because it might mean betraying Alec. Do you see what I mean?" She spoke very quietly, but the quality of her spirit showed through. "I could say yes, and mean it, but if Alec is alive, if he's giving away these secrets, I might not be able to bring myself to tell you. How would that help you, then?"

Merrick said slowly: "I think you'd tell us, Judy." He meant that; in fact he meant more, he was sure that she would do this thing. "But you've still time to decide. We ought to go back to London at once. As soon as we're there, you can make up your mind. Right?"

"Yes," she said, very quietly. "I—"

She didn't finish, for there was a tap at the door.

It opened, and Arden came in.

13

TOUCH AND GO

Arden came further in, leaving the door open behind him, and Judy just dropped on to the couch, as if the strength had gone out of her legs. Merrick turned to face the man slowly, but kept his hands in sight.

For behind Arden was the man Kip.

Arden was dressed in a light grey suit of immaculate cut, the familiar razor edge creases, brown brogue shoes which shone brightly; a dandy of a man. He had no briefcase.

"Good evening, Mrs. Ryall," he said formally, and nodded to Merrick. "Evening, Merrick."

Kip, at the door, smiled broadly; and showed the gap in his big teeth.

"Of course, you're both surprised," Arden went on. "You wouldn't expect me to walk in as brazenly as this, would you?" He didn't actually laugh, but it was almost as if he said: "Ha-ha." He was brusque, business-like. "The unexpected is the thing that usually gets results; if you and Craigie would be unorthodox at times, instead of sticking to the normal methods, you might do better." He glanced at Merrick again, disdainfully. "Mrs. Ryall, you're under no obligation, but are quite free to come away with me—to see your husband."

He did not even smile.

Merrick said slowly: "Mrs. Ryall stays here."

"I really don't want to have to argue with you," said Arden irritably. "Mrs. Ryall is old enough to make up her own mind. As I say, she is under no obligation, but her husband would like to see her—that's understandable enough, isn't it? Here in Switzerland, Merrick and the Department he serves have no jurisdiction, no influence of any kind. He cannot stop you from leaving with me, Mrs. Ryall, so it's entirely up to you."

Judy looked sharply at Merrick, then at Kip. The small man came in slowly. He wore a Tyrolean hat with a coloured feather in the band, an open-necked shirt of bright green, and a Swiss type jacket, with a belt at the back and big pockets. His khaki trousers and brown woollen stockings emphasised the size of his feet, which were as big as his hands in proportion. He looked bronzed and well, and ugly and menacing.

He rubbed his hands together.

Judy caught her breath.

"And when does Mrs. Ryall have to make up her mind?" Merrick asked sarcastically.

"At once, naturally—we can give her half an hour to pack. You aren't being kept here against your will, Mrs. Ryall, are you? These fine *gentlemen* wouldn't do such a thing, would they?" The sneer was half-hearted; he seemed too impatient to worry much about what he said. "What is your decision, Mrs. Ryall?"

Judy said: "Where is my husband?"

"I can't tell you that just now, but I can assure you that he is quite well again, fully recovered from his accident, and most anxious to see you."

"How do I know that's the truth?"

"Oh, come, come," said Arden impatiently, "what point is there in my coming here and lying to you? After all, there is a risk. Merrick here is known to be impetuous and quite a good shot, and he is doubtless armed. There are several more of his friends within call, I've no doubt. But I did not think you were likely to come at the behest of an underling."

Kip grinned.

"But I hoped that when I came in person, you would understand that I was quite serious," Arden went on. "Haven't you had a letter from your husband?"

"Yes," Judy said, slowly.

"Then, my dear good woman, why ask foolish questions?" Arden demanded, and sounded almost angry. "We're not children. I suppose you've seen rather too much of the puerilities of men like Merrick. The simple question is this, Mrs. Ryall— do you want to come with me and rejoin your husband, or don't you? He would be distressed if you didn't, I've no doubt, but I can't help that."

Judy didn't answer.

Merrick tried to guess what the answer would be: and to guess at what thoughts were passing through her mind. She had overcome the repulsion which she felt for Kip, who stood rubbing his big, ugly hands together; hands which had once tried to break her lovely neck.

"Mrs. Ryall, *please!*" Arden almost shouted.

She said quietly: "I am going back to London with Mr. Merrick in a day or two. I shall go to my flat. If Alec joins me there, I shall obviously know that he's alive. If he asks me to join him somewhere else, I'll know what to say. But I won't come with you."

Arden raised a hand, forefinger pointing.

"You are making a big mistake. It might not be possible for

your husband to join you. I am taking a big enough risk myself. He—"

"Don't shout at me!" Judy snapped.

Arden broke off, as if startled, blinked, then shrugged his shoulders. He turned to Merrick. The impression of a man who was quite something in the City had never been stronger.

"If I were you, I should persuade her to change her mind, Merrick," he said. "Meanwhile, you can give Craigie a message for me. He is wasting his time. The trouble with Department Z is very simple—it's out-dated and out-moded. All its activities are based on age-old methods, but spying and counter-espionage have changed. Tell him that we use different methods. We're a large organisation, of course, and have access to the most up-to-date scientific methods. I'll grant you this, it was quickly obvious that Department Z was the only group worth worrying about, the rest of M.I.5" —he shrugged, and gave a little, almost puckish grin— "well, really! And some of the counter-espionage of the other countries was really too juvenile for words. You gave us plenty to think about, but we got your measure at last, and we shall break you, little by little. In fact I wrote and told Craigie so, but you can emphasise the message. We know the Department, its agents, its methods, its activities. We shall kill or otherwise cause the defection of agent after agent, and whenever you attack us, we shall be most severe. But we've no objection to the Department working against other espionage groups."

Merrick made himself say: "Nice of you."

Arden waved a hand.

"It isn't a question of being nice." The man was so pompous that he was unbelievable. "It's a simple matter of business. The Vandermin Group, as we might call ourselves, doesn't intend to be harassed by Department Z. If you will lay off us, however, and concentrate on other spies and espionage organisations, then we shall leave you alone. We don't want this kind of warfare, we don't particularly want to smash the reputation of Department Z, but if you get in our way—"

"You just brush us aside," Merrick said, and found it easier to speak.

"Exactly." Arden nodded portentously. "I'm glad that you understand. Now—Kip." His voice changed, slightly.

"Okay," Kip said.

His hands moved, and he flashed an automatic from his pocket. It appeared so swiftly that it took Merrick completely by surprise. The gun covered him. His heart began to pound.

"Don't move, brother," said Kip softly.

"Mrs. Ryall, you're coming with us," Arden said. "Now don't be alarmed, we shan't hurt you. I confess that we would have done before, but not now. We want to take you to your husband, he is so very fond of you. I'm afraid there won't be time to pack any clothes, but that is your own fault." He took her wrist. "Come along. Merrick, give my message to Craigie, emphasise that I am prepared to live and let live."

"Jim!" Judy exclaimed. "Don't let—"

"Oh, come along," said Arden irritably, "why will you always be so obstinate? It won't get you anywhere. Merrick, I don't want to kill you. I've friends nearby, watching the chalet and guarding the cable car. As soon as we've gone down, we shall put it out of order, and you won't be able to follow us. The only other way down takes nearly a day. Just stay where you are. Kip, give me five minutes. Hurry—you are an exasperating woman!" he added in a sharp voice, and pushed Judy towards the passage.

No one else appeared.

"Nice weather," Kip said, and grinned again. The revolver looked small in his hand. "Okay, Joshua."

Merrick said: "Arden—"

Arden gave Judy another push, and disappeared.

It was the moment to use the one weapon Merrick had and which the others wouldn't expect. Merrick judged the distance between himself and Kip; two yards. He couldn't swing an arm and take a chance that he would be able to knock the gun aside—but he could spring.

He heard Arden call: "Open the door."

Merrick sprang.

It was as if there were springs in his heels, and he was on Kip before the man realised that it was possible. Kip could shoot then; or be delayed for the split second that mattered because of shock. He lost his chance. Merrick crashed into him, Kip went backwards like a log, his hat fell off, he banged his head against the wooden floor.

Merrick stamped on his wrist; the gun fell from nerveless fingers. Merrick kicked it and it slid along the floor, bent down and smacked Kip on the temple with the butt of his own gun.

He leapt to the door.

The front door was open, and the bright evening light came through. A man stood on the veranda, as Joshua Arden and Judy reached the top of the steps. Arden was so confident that no one would follow them that he didn't look round.

Merrick fired at the man behind Arden; and then fired at Arden. He saw one fall, the other stagger.

Arden lost his grip on Judy's hand.

"Judy! Back here!" Merrick shouted.

She turned her head, then swung round and raced back towards the door. Arden staggered against the rail by the steps, holding a foot off the ground. Then other men appeared, armed; a shot hummed through the doorway, could have missed Judy only by a fraction.

"Door!" roared Merrick.

Judy kept her wits about her, she was superb. She slammed the door, and as it closed, a bullet thudded into it. Here, in the hall, there were only two small windows; Merrick grabbed the girl and pulled her against the wall. He heard two more shots, and then some confused shouting. He knew the chalet inside out; and the safest place was upstairs, in one of the attic rooms. The danger, if danger there were, would come when they passed the huge landing window—but Arden and his men seemed to be at the front of the house, not the back.

"Stairs," he said, and pushed her towards them, then backed after her, covering the front door with the gun. No one seemed to be on the veranda, but there was shooting outside; the unmistakable barking of pistol shots. He reached the stairs, and Judy was half-way up.

"Jim—"

"Attic room, and—"

A new sound broke across his words, of footsteps inside the house. The servants? The footsteps were light and hurried, coming along a passage which led from the kitchen; there were two men at least.

"Upstairs," he breathed, and heard Judy moving away from him. He stood close to the wall, where he could cover the passage leading from the kitchen; and his gun was trained on it.

The footsteps stopped.

He knew that the men were near, and that they were wary; they probably expected him. He glanced up at the landing. Judy was pressing close against the wooden wall, out of sight of the window; she seemed never to lose her head.

A man called: "Anyone about? You wouldn't be alive Jim, would you?"

It was Elliott.

14

LONDON AGAIN

Merrick leaned against the wall, tension easing, gun drooping; there was no mistaking Elliott's voice.

"Unearthly silence," Elliott said to whoever was with him. "I hope they haven't been dispatched to the hereafter, as I've heard it called. Jim needed a little spiritual preparation. Jim—"

"Okay," Merrick called clearly.

From that moment on, the shock ebbed out of his system; he knew not only what had happened, but what they had to try to do. He ran down the stairs, calling: "Stay there, Judy!" He was in the hall when Elliott appeared. Even the sight of Elliott's appearance did nothing to stop him, although Elliott had a deerstalker hat and looked as if he were a mountaineer dressed for a late Victorian assault on the Matterhorn.

"Jim—"

"Must stop Arden," Merrick gasped. "One man's in there, look after him." He ran towards the door.

Elliott moved as if electrified, and ran after him. He reached the door first, and landed against it heavily, his back at the door, facing Merrick. He beamed, and his big moustache spread out, looking bushier than ever.

"Caution strongly recommended," he declared. "The war is on outside, and we love you too much to want to lose you."

"Arden's there, we want him."

"Oh, I couldn't agree more. Only he isn't alone. Open the door," invited Elliott, "but not with your customary impetuous haste. As you would if you knew that a Bisley winner or Buffalo Bill was a couple of hundred yards away, waiting to pick you off."

Merrick didn't speak.

He heard the man who had been with Elliott go into the room where Kip was, and called out: "Be careful." Elliott grinned; Merrick caught sight of his white teeth, and chuckled in spite of himself. Then he opened the door stealthily.

He knew what Elliott meant then.

Three men were crouching near the hut which housed the cable car. Two carried rifles. Arden was limping towards the hut, the door of which was open. Suddenly, one of the men levelled the gun, but not towards the chalet; the shot roared.

"Two more of our chaps outside, at the back," Elliott remarked. "I hope they don't lose their top-knots. Nice chaps. I know, Jim, we could do a bit of shooting, but the odds are against us and I'm not sure we ought to take any more risks to get Arden"

Merrick growled: "We ought to try."

But he knew that it was useless anyhow. Arden was actually disappearing into the hut, and two of the men covering him were backing into it. The third wasn't far away.

Two shots rang out.

Suddenly the third man disappeared into the hut.

"Of course we could fire on 'em from up here while they're going down in the cage." Elliott took the words out of

Merrick's mouth. "But that might not please the Swiss authorities, and Gordon asked me to cause as little fuss as possible. We don't want to lose our convalescent chalet, do we, but we couldn't blame anyone for turfing us out if they thought that this kind of schemozzle was likely to happen often. Let's go and see if anyone's hurt."

Merrick said: "And let Arden go?"

Elliott stood very still. His eyes were a steely grey. He looked more mature; an older man. All the facetiousness dropped away, and his voice was hard and unrelenting.

"Yes, Jim. I'm in charge. My considered opinion is that we should. I'll take any kicks."

Merrick said slowly: "Well, all right."

He stepped on to the veranda, and saw two men hurrying down from the cover of some rocks towards the chalet. They were too far away to reach the cable before it stopped.

Merrick went briskly towards it. From half-way down the slope, about the spot where he had met Judy, he could see the big cage going down the wire rope; the cage would carry six or seven people. Arden was sitting down, only just visible because the other three were standing in front of him, obviously to protect him if there were any shooting. The cable spanned a narrow valley, but there was a long drop into rocky land. The cage was moving over the valley now. At the far end two men were waiting; and near them, on the rough road which led to the main road, some miles away, an American car stood in the shadows. The sun was setting, and down in the valley dusk had already fallen.

The cage moved swiftly.

Merrick waited until it reached the ground. The others climbed out, then Arden was carried towards the car. That was something, and Arden wouldn't forget this in a hurry.

How had he come?

What point was there in asking questions?

Merrick walked back towards the chalet. Then two men came out of it, and he stopped abruptly.

One was Corlett; the other, Jim Ross. He fought down his prejudice against Corlett, and saluted brightly. He was in no mood for the Department's vernacular, but forced himself to say:

"We could jump across the valley."

"You could," Corlett said. "We're not workers of miracles ourselves." Did he mean to be offensive? "As they've cut the telephone wire, that's our best hope. Handy at that, aren't they?"

"Elementary, my dear Watson," Merrick said.

He went into the chalet, leaving the two outside. He heard Elliott's voice. He hadn't seen Elliott before except as a vacant-looking, absurdly unreal figure—and his dress now was part of the act. But he wouldn't forget the look in Elliott's eyes for a long time, and he could easily understand why Craigie called Elliott good.

Merrick went into the little room.

Elliott was drinking a cup of tea. Judy sat on the couch. Kip had gone, the room was tidied, nothing indicated what had happened; and Merrick remembered again how quickly the signs of a raid could vanish.

"They gone?" asked Elliott, as if for the sake of it.

"Yes."

"Did a good job," Elliott said. "We have to hand it to 'em, Jim. They attacked two ways—up the cable, and over the mountains. The mountain party must have started off yesterday morning to get here in time. Took us from the rear, of course, but we were watching." He lit a cigarette; and looked in danger of setting his moustache alight. "We must hand it to Arden for cool nerve, too. Just came up in the cage with a bland smile and walked up to the front door. Used strong-arm stuff for the staff, but no one's badly hurt. Unless you are."

"I'm all right."

"And we've a prisoner, too," Elliott said, with a note of satisfaction. "We won't let this one go in a hurry. Mrs. Ryall says it's the chap who nearly choked the life out of her, but she is prepared to forego all personal reprisals." Here he was, the silly ass again. "We're stuck here for the night, I'm afraid, but one of our chaps is already on his way down—to the nearest telephone, I mean. We'll have cable engineers along in the morning, and life will be normal. Meanwhile, anyone feeling hungry?"

"What's happened to Kip?"

"I've given him a shot of morphia to keep him quiet," Elliott said. "Tackle him later. Not that I think he's much of a talker—do you?"

"He could be."

Elliott shrugged. "We'll see. I wish Loftus were here, he knows how to ask the questions. You know, Jim, I *am* getting hungry," he added almost peevishly. "Missed tea and all that. I'll go and see what happened to the cook."

He went out.

Judy said unexpectedly: "He's—odd, isn't he?"

"We're all odd," Merrick said, with an effort. "Elliott's all right. It's a strain. As if you didn't know!" He went moodily to the window. "I think he made a mistake in not trying to hold Arden, but I suppose it was wise." He paused, and then looked into her eyes, and she met his frankly. "Why didn't you go with Arden?"

"You don't mean that, do you?" she asked. "You really mean—do I believe Arden about Alec?"

Merrick shrugged.

"I don't know what to believe and I don't know what to do," Judy said. "There's just one thing—I can't believe that Alec has turned traitor."

But her tone and her eyes told that she was already beginning to doubt.

The man named Kip came round from the drug a little after midnight. Elliott, Merrick and Corlett questioned him. They didn't pull their punches, and didn't get a squeak out of the man. Short of third degree, they never would.

They telephoned Craigie.

"Get Kip back here as soon as you can," Craigie said.

Two men were on duty during the night, but nothing more happened. Merrick did not think that another attempt would be made on the chalet.

He slept well, once he did get off, but woke early. He was out of the bathroom and dressing when there was a tap at the door; probably morning tea. He put on a dressing-gown, and called: "Come in."

Judy came.

Merrick's eyes lit up.

She wore the same clothes as yesterday, with a cream-coloured swagger coat, for protection against the morning chill which the wind brought down from the snow-clad mountains.

"Hallo, Jim."

"Couldn't you sleep, either?"

"Not late," she said. "Jim, I've been trying to get everything clear, and I think I have. I'll help you. That is—" she spoke very quietly, and her eyes were on his all the time, as if she were willing him to believe that she was trying so desperately to be honest. "I'm going to try to help. I can't be sure what I'll feel like if—if I find that Alec is alive and working for them."

Merrick said gruffly: "Can't you? I can."

117

She didn't answer.

There were a dozen things Merrick wanted to say, but only one that he should. He had to brief her. He had to tell her what to do if she were caught; kidnapped; in the power of the other side.

She listened calmly.

"You may have a chance to telephone a message," Merrick said. "Just call any police station and ask them to give the message to Z. It'll reach us. Clear?"

"Yes," she said.

"If you can't get to a telephone, use this stuff," Merrick went on. "It looks like face powder." He handed her two cellophane packets, not much larger than postage stamps. "Tear a corner and shake the stuff out of a window, a car, anywhere in the open air. It will spread and turn a bright red or a bright green. The green is for 'Alec's alive', the red if he's dead."

Judy said: "I see."

"The police have orders to look for and report it anywhere," Merrick said. "And one of these tiny packets is enough at any one time."

There were a dozen smaller packets in each, small enough to hide in lipstick, compact; anywhere.

"God bless," Merrick said, abruptly.

Merrick looked out of the tiny window by his side, over the vast sprawling mass of London which lay beneath him. It stretched so far in all directions that it was hard to believe that these were all buildings made by the hand of man. The roads and streets looked like the threads of some gigantic, disorderly spider's web; or as if a million spiders had spun their webs at the same time, each spinning a different pattern.

The sun shone upon the fair face of England.

Merrick looked across at Judy, who was at a window on the other side. Sensing his gaze, she turned, smiled, and said:

"It's unbelievable."

"Not bad."

"How long do you think we'll be?"

"Oh, ten or fifteen minutes, I'd say," Merrick said. "Perhaps less, as we're losing height. London airport is over there." He pointed; but the sun was reflecting on too many roofs and windows for him to be sure which great open space was the airport. They were still at seven or eight thousand feet, and the two engines were turning over smoothly.

It was a twenty-one-seater passenger aircraft on special charter.

Elliott, Corlett and the other Z men were nearer the flight deck, each at a window seat. They were smoking, but any moment now instructions would come over the loudspeaker for them to put out their cigarettes.

It was forty-eight hours since Arden had come to the chalet.

The rescue party had arrived the following morning, and everything had gone smoothly. No one at the chalet had been seriously hurt. No one had reported what had happened to the Swiss authorities, so there would be no scandal.

Kip still hadn't talked.

He was also on the plane, in a drugged sleep. He had made no attempt to cause trouble when being brought aboard, and had passed through the Swiss customs without any difficulty.

They had doped him half an hour ago.

The flight had been smooth; Merrick hadn't had much to say; Judy had been quiet, too. Neither had talked much since she had agreed to serve the Department.

But Merrick could not clear his mind of all that it meant.

At moments he wished that he could be taken off the job for fear that emotion would get the better of him; at others, he knew that if he were taken off until it was over, he would hate himself.

His thoughts switched from one thing to the other, but always came back to one question; how desperate was the threat from Vandermin? Was it a serious menace to the Department?

He saw the door leading to the flight deck open, one of the crew came out, went to Elliott, and talked to him earnestly. Merrick watched; Judy was as interested. The officer went back, and Elliott promptly got up and came towards them. He was smiling cheerfully, so probably there was nothing much wrong. The parting in his moustache showed up clearly, a trick of light.

"Not landing at London," he said briefly. "We've been diverted to Croydon. Just had it over the air."

"Doesn't make much difference," Merrick said quickly.

"Oh, no. Nearer, if anything." Elliott dropped into the seat next to Judy: "Not a bad flight in this old kite. Like flying?"

"Not much," she admitted.

"Sick?"

"No, I just don't enjoy it when the plane sways or drops," Judy gave a little laugh, was almost embarrassed; Merrick marvelled again at her candour. "I'm scared—never happy until I'm really on the ground again, and I hate taking off and landing."

"This thing's as gentle as a kitten," said Elliott. "And on a day like this, nothing could go wrong—eh, Jim?"

"Impossible," Merrick agreed warmly.

"Oh, don't take me seriously," Judy said.

"No one ever does," Corlett said from behind them.

Judy did not seem nervous of anything but the landing. Merrick was nervous of plenty. He guessed why they had been diverted; so did the others. Craigie believed that there was danger in landing at London Airport. A reception party awaited them there.

Would Croydon be safe?

Merrick was more on edge than usual, but anxious to hide the fact from Judy. Elliott had soon gone to join the other men. Judy watched the sprawling mass below, drawing nearer as they circled, ready to land. They could soon pick out the airport, the little red brick houses nearby, the factories too. Then, almost before they realised it, they went in for the landing run. Merrick saw Judy stiffen, but she didn't look round, or look away from the flashing earth.

They touched down, bumped a little, then slowed, down; before long they were taxi-ing.

Merrick grinned with relief, but the other fear remained with the need to watch everyone; everything.

"All over," he said.

"I know I'm silly." Judy's naturalness had never seemed more appealing. "Well, we won't be long now! Shall I be seeing these leaders of yours—the one Arden called Craigie?"

"I expect so."

Merrick helped her down the steps. Elliott was watching at the foot; and he also waited while Kip was brought out on a stretcher. Elliott was still in charge; and Merrick didn't mind. He had plenty to think about. It wouldn't be long before the idyll with Judy would be over completely. They had virtually lived together for three months, which proved that they could live well together and not get on each other's nerves.

They'd been diverted from London airport.

The two things clashed, all the time; he was never in complete control of his thoughts. He would have to find a way to beat off the emotional pull; in a moment of crisis, that might be deadly. He tried to watch Judy dispassionately as they passed through customs, then went outside the airport building to the car. It looked like a taxi—one of the old black Daimlers, with a square body, a glass partition inside and a fat speaking tube. Merrick knew that the Department often used that kind of cab; it had a Hackney Carriage plate up, and looked as innocuous as anything could.

Merrick didn't know the driver, who was in uniform.

Elliott left Corlett and the other Department men with Kip, to leave in another large car, and joined Merrick and Judy. In this get-up, he had looked ridiculous in the Swiss mountains; he looked an anachronism here, but was not even slightly self-conscious.

"Mind if I keep you company?" he almost burbled. "We're to go straight to the office."

"Why should I mind?" Merrick asked. And grinned. "Arden said that we were old-fashioned and out-moded, and he probably meant archaic, too. I can see what he means."

"Unkind," protested Elliott, with a straight face. "Shift over, there's plenty of room."

The seat was high, and Judy sat between the two men. Merrick felt his leg against hers; her hand against his. He tried not to look at her all the time, but sensed that she was aware of the intensity of his feeling. He found himself wondering if they would ever be on such terms as these again.

He felt—tired.

Elliott yawned.

The big car sped through the suburbs of London, jolting and jogging—and it wasn't until he was almost asleep that Merrick realised that this wasn't natural, that he should be wide awake, but was losing consciousness.

15

KIDNAPPED

Elliott!" Merrick shouted in sudden alarm. "Elliott!"

"Jim—" Judy said; and she looked and sounded scared as she woke with a start. "What's the matter?"

"Elliott!" Merrick bellowed; he leaned across Judy and shook Elliott savagely; but he couldn't use much vigour, he hadn't really the strength; sleep was coming over him in waves. "Judy, wake him up, wake him!" He edged forward on his seat and banged at the glass partition; there was little strength in his banging, he was nearly under.

The chauffeur looked straight ahead, taking no notice.

They were inside-streets, where few people were about, travelling at nearly forty miles an hour, faster than they should in a built-up area. Merrick tried to shout again, but the shout turned into a yawn, and his fist slid down the smooth glass.

"Jim, what is it?" He could just hear Judy's voice, as if from a long way off. His head was whirling, he could see two chauffeurs, two caps, two Judys, two lots of pavement on each side. "What's happening to us?"

"Stop the car!" he bellowed.

It went on.

He turned to look at Judy. She was as scared as anyone could be. Her lips were parted, her eyes told him what she felt. Then she yawned.

"Jim, what is it? I can't keep awake!"

He knew that she was seeing everything double, as he was. He tried to bang on the partition, but a child could have exerted more strength; in any case the chauffeur didn't intend to hear.

The speaking tube—he could shout into that, might be heard on the pavement. Merrick turned his head and found the tube close to Elliott, who was leaning forward, chin on his chest, breathing gustily and stirring the big moustache.

Of course, gas was coming through the speaking tube.

Merrick touched the handle of the door and pulled at it but found that it wouldn't move. He mouthed at two women who were standing and talking on the pavement as the car flashed past, and saw the women break off their conversation to stare after him. The car passed a policeman on a bicycle, and Merrick shouted with his mouth wide open; the shout turned into a yawn that hurt his jaws.

"Judy—" he began, desperately, and turned to her.

She had fallen asleep.

"Judy!" He snatched at her hand—but she took no notice. She was dead to the world. He knew that he would be, soon. His head seemed to be swelling, swelling, getting like a huge balloon, grotesque and yet painful, ugly, round, painful, swelling.

Swelling . . .

Getting dark.

"Now wake up, sir," a man said in a clear, patient voice. "You can't stay there all day, you know. Wake up, sir."

Merrick felt a hand at his shoulder, shaking him; and then felt daylight strike at his eyes. He had no recollection at all, at that moment.

"Drunk?" another man said.

"Don't smell anything," said the first. "Two of 'em. Both in the back, that's funny." He shook Merrick's shoulder again, more vigorously. "Now wake up, sir, please."

"Eh?" muttered Merrick, vaguely aware that something was expected of him. "Am awake." He tried to get up, but his head was heavy and his limbs were lethargic. "Wake," he muttered. "Who're you? Where—am I?"

"Little place near Coulsdon, sir," said the man, and only one kind of man would keep calling him 'sir'; a policeman. Merrick opened his eyes wider, and sure enough a policeman stood by the open door of a car, leaning inside, his helmet on one side, likely to fall off at any moment but for the restraining hold of the black chin strap. "Now wake up, please."

"Must be drunk," said the man behind him—a small man, leaning on a bicycle. "Blotto."

"Well, there's no smell," repeated the constable.

"Smell," echoed Merrick. For some reason the word annoyed him; and then he began to remember. He glanced round, and terror struck at him—and stayed.

Elliott was in the other corner, still breathing heavily, his moustache moving up and down. But Judy had gone. Dear, precious Judy, whose hand had been touching his, who had been with him for three months, who—

"Here, steady," said the constable, in sudden alarm. "Look out, Bert, he's going to faint."

"Blotto, that's what he—"

Merrick gritted his teeth, felt his head going round and round again, knew that the policeman wasn't far wrong; but he fought back the nausea, beat it, and turned to face the man. Too many things were racing through his mind at the same time, and he knew that he had to say something intelligible. He felt choked; and gradually realised that his pallor was enough to alarm the two men.

He said very carefully and distinctly: "We must get in touch with—Scotland Yard—at once." He knew that he could show his card but wasn't sure there was any need. "Superintendent—Miller. I had better—telephone myself."

"Not just yet, sir, you're a bit under the weather still. What happened here? We've been told you've been parked under these trees for the past two hours—thought I'd better make sure everything was okay. Talk about sleep!"

"Yes," said Merrick, very carefully. "I see what you mean. But I'm all right and must speak to Scotland Yard." He forced a smile. "Special—work."

"Well, if you must, sir."

"Blotto," said the man named Bert, knowingly. "Don't let him fool you."

"Let me—get out," Merrick said.

The constable helped him. He swayed, then leaned heavily against the side of the car. They were beneath trees at the side of a narrow country road. The trees, all beech and birch, were full of tiny leaves. They rustled and seemed to sing beneath the bright sun, and their green had a translucent beauty. A long way off, there was a valley and green fields, and above was the clear blue sky and the warm light.

"Where's the—nearest—telephone?"

"Well, I expect we could use one at a house just along the road," said the constable. "But—"

"It's vital, I tell you." Merrick fought back a temptation to shout. "Seriously, I must—"

"Bert, you look after that chap," the constable said, decisively at last. "I'll take this gentleman to a house where he can telephone."

Bert sniffed.

It was a narrow, winding road, and the modern house, timbered and with white walls, came as a surprise to Merrick. There was a big black retriever, and a golden-haired girl of four or five and a lean, neatly-dressed, youthful woman rather like Mrs. Gilmour, his neighbour. The telephone was in a square hall. He sat at it. The constable said something about a cup of hot tea, and the woman disappeared. Merrick telephoned Scotland Yard; there was a noticeable thawing of the constable's manner when he actually dialled Whitehall 1212.

Miller, the liaison officer between the Yard and Department Z, wasn't in; but his second-in-command was. When Merrick introduced himself, the man said sharply:

"Jim Merrick! Thank the Lord one of you is all right. Is Elliott—"

"Yes," said Merrick. "Yes, he's all right. He's doped but he'll come round. Judy—"

"We know about Judy Ryall," the man said. "You go to Whitehall as soon as you can, and I'll telephone the office."

"How did you know about Judy?" Anything to do with Judy mattered desperately. "Is she—"

"Arden telephoned, just to gloat, I fancy," said the Yard man. "The car was held up and your driver shanghaied, another man put in his place. We've found the original driver, and he's not hurt much. You may as well know it all—that chap you collected, Kip or something, has gone too. But we'd better not waste time."

"No," Merrick muttered. "No. Good-bye."

So the whole thing had been known, he thought, as he sat in a small dining-room with the sun shining through mullioned window, sipping hot, sweet tea. They had been diverted from one airfield to another, but the pressure hadn't eased Vandermin's men from fooling them. That was the dreadful, the terrifying part; that they could get away with all this so easily. It was as if all the methods which the Department used had become worthless.

What would Craigie say?

Or Loftus—

And where was Judy?

Thought of her was like an agonising wound.

Merrick walked up the stone steps in the building off Whitehall. He pressed his fingernail into the tiny groove. He went into the square cubby hole when the sliding door opened. He waited. Another door slid open, and he stepped through, passing Loftus. He saw Loftus, of course, but it was Craigie on whom his eyes first focussed—and sight of Craigie which shocked him out of his mood of defeatism, almost of despair.

Craigie was *old.*

It was three months since Merrick had seen his Chief, and the change was so startling that it drove everything else out of his mind, including Judy. 'Old' was the only word. Craigie's hair was snow white. His face had twice as many wrinkles as it had a few months ago. He was standing up, and his shoulders, usually so square, sagged heavily. He looked at Merrick, and at Elliott behind him, with eyes which had always seemed tired but now seemed as if the life had been drawn out of them.

Was that true?

Merrick drew nearer, and began to recover from the shock. There was still a glint in those eyes, a hint of purpose; and to his surprise, when Craigie shook hands his grip was firm.

But the change was—appalling.

What had caused it?

16

DISASTER?

"Come and sit down, Jim," Craigie said, and at least his voice hadn't changed. "It's good to see you looking so well." He waved to one of the armchairs, but Merrick didn't sit down, just stood and looked at his Chief. Craigie's lips dropped in a smile which was also reminiscent of the man as Merrick remembered him. "Shocked as all that, are you?"

Merrick said quietly: "Yes."

"You haven't seen it developing gradually," Craigie remarked dryly. He picked up a meerschaum and began to play with the bowl. "It isn't all caused by events, either. I've picked up some bug that isn't doing me any good."

"Or been given one," Elliott said sharply. He had recovered more slowly than Merrick from the dope, but half-way to Whitehall from Coulsdon, he had shown that he was feeling much better. He still looked tired and pale, but his voice was steady and his manner decisive. "Just another of Vandermin's little tricks," he added.

Merrick took out cigarettes and handed them round.

"Possibly," he said heavily. "Have we ever *seen* Vandermin? Do we know he exists? Is he more than a name?"

No one answered.

"Well, is he?" Merrick asked abruptly. "I don't know, but I've lived with the name for years, it's seemed, but as for catching a glimpse of him—never a hope." He sat carefully on the arm of a chair, and looked round at the others. He had to sheer away from thought of this change in Craigie, for the man was breaking up. The possibility that Elliott was right, and that 'Vandermin' was responsible, was already snarling at him. If Vandermin could get at the head of the Department—

"He's a name," Craigie said, "and he's a description. Two of our men, now in the little black book, believed that they saw him, and gave a description. Each tallied with that of the man who called himself Arden." Obviously Craigie still had a complete grasp of what was going on; his mental faculties hadn't been impaired; but his cheeks were hollow, his bones pressed against the skin, it was almost a skull of a face. "There's no need to go into detail. I was satisfied that a man calling himself Vandermin existed. It was after secret papers had been stolen from Harwell and another lot from a jet aircraft factory. We traced both sets of documents to Vandermin, or to the man they described and called Vandermin—but before they could give us any more details, they were killed."

Merrick growled: "And that's all?"

"Not quite all. We know that there's a continual bubble of spying activity. As a Department we keep close to most of it. Half—three-quarters—of the information which the spies get, we either get back or trace to its new home. Most of it goes to countries overseas. But what happens to the stuff we lose without any trace? Who buys it? We've often traced stolen secrets back to someone who could be Vandermin. The information certainly isn't used elsewhere, as far as we know.

Remember that we lost some papers from a bacteriological experimental station five months ago, Jim? That was the job you were on before this."

"I remember."

"Within a month, we knew that it was being studied in Moscow," Craigie told him. "In practically every case before Vandermin appeared on the scene, we knew where the secrets were going—Moscow, Buenos Aires, Calcutta—or if it comes to that, New York or Paris. I'm making it very clear, to show you why we put down to Vandermin anything we can't trace home. He's almost a composite creature. And he has possession of a host of vital documents. As an individual, a unit or a syndicate, he's not just dynamite, he's atomic."

"Reasonable," Elliott said, and smoothed his moustache. He looked unexpectedly hopeful. "You wouldn't be one of those low types who keeps beer on the premises, would you?"

"On the floor in the cupboard," Loftus answered. "Help yourself and then help the rest of us."

"Oh, good show." Elliott moved to the cupboard which held everything. "Where's Roy Corlett? Any news?"

"Found in a garden, unhurt," said Craigie. "Kip had vanished, of course. Everything they do is to make us laughing stocks."

"Yes," Elliott agreed, and added lightly: "Gordon, are you sure that Corlett's reliable?"

It wasn't a sensation. There was hardly a pause before Craigie said quietly: "I've stopped trusting anyone."

"I can believe it," Merrick broke in harshly. He made himself go on: "What's been happening since I went for my holiday?"

Craigie had filled his pipe, and was lighting it; he puffed with the old vigour, it was like looking at an animated skull.

"The catalepsy business faded out. No prisoner has talked.

Vandermin, through Arden, can do more or less what he likes. He's as cool as they come, and seems quite fearless." He paused. "The situation couldn't be much worse, Jim. Vandermin seems to be able to put a finger on us whenever he likes. He doesn't always do so. Most jobs we get we handle as we always did, without trouble. But certain jobs lead to—" Craigie paused, drew at the pipe until the tobacco glowed red, and then looked straight into Merrick's eyes— "disaster," he finished deliberately.

"And we mean disaster," Elliott declared, emerging with two large bottles of beer.

"As to-day," said Craigie simply. "Our moves are all anticipated. We knew that London Airport was being watched by Vandermin's men—we've a list of some of them. So for safety's sake, we diverted you. No one hostile was anywhere near Croydon, as far as we knew. We had the taxi followed by another agent on a motor-bicycle, one not likely to be suspected, but both the driver and the motor-cyclist were attacked, and dealt with—and you know what happened. It's like an uncanny anticipation of what we're going to do next, but—" Craigie broke off, shrugging.

Elliott, having dived again, re-appeared with four pewter tankards.

"Who likes a nice head?" he asked.

Merrick forced down a surge of irritation.

"It's worse," Loftus broke in. "We have nine places in London where you fellows can meet, all of which are supposed to be secret. Seven of them have been visited by Vandermin's men. They even leave a sign—a V sign!" He threw his arms up into the air. "Sardonic devils!"

"Beer," said Elliott, and brought round the tankards, handling them with a skill which could only have come from long practice. "Hoist with our own petard, as it were. We used to be running around putting salt on their tails, and now they're putting it on ours. But don't make the picture one of complete gloom, Gordon."

Merrick took his tankard.

The beer looked good and had a nice head, but he felt flat; as if the life had been driven out of him. It was only partly because Judy had disappeared; the appearance of Craigie followed by this story of unparalleled disaster, made up the rest. The thought that there might be a bright side hadn't entered his head. He looked expectantly, hopefully, at Craigie; surely Craigie would have said if there were any reason to hope that the end was in sight.

"It isn't all gloomy," Craigie agreed. "We've several new hide-outs, and agents we're pretty sure that Vandermin doesn't know. We're trying to match bluff by bluff." One of the words which mattered most, hurt most, was 'trying'; at any other time, Craigie would have said simply: "We are matching bluff by bluff." He paused to draw at his pipe, thinking very carefully over his words. "For instance, we've traced Arden and his wife to another home. We aren't sure that Alec is at the same place—we've no reason to think he is—but he might be. We've allowed Arden to escape deliberately, so that he could be followed, and we haven't failed all the time—he's been traced home from Switzerland. We even know that he's in bed with his leg wounds."

"Nice work!" Elliott enthused. "Wizzo!"

"Where?" Merrick asked abruptly.

"At a house in the country not far from St. Albans," Craigie told him. "We've been watching it closely. I don't think that Arden realises that, certainly he hasn't done anything to suggest that he does, and he's still using the place." That remark hurt, too; it showed how Craigie's confidence had weakened, a few months ago he would have been sure that

Arden knew nothing. Now Arden, or Vandermin, or whoever it was, could play cat-and-mouse with Craigie and with Department Z; that was the incredible thing.

"Dear old boy," said Elliott and gulped down his beer. "Then what are we doing here?"

Merrick's momentary irritation faded. Elliott was as much on edge as he; under that silly ass façade, he was anxious, as desperate as anyone. He hadn't Merrick's driving desire to find Judy, that was all.

Craigie said briskly: "We've got to make sure that we don't throw anything away. This thing has crept up on us for a long time, and finally galloped past us. We can almost say that we're fighting for our existence as a Department. We have to think of that first, must forget the urgency of the different espionage jobs being carried out under our noses. Whether we like it, whether the Government likes it or not, we are the only effective counter-espionage group in the country. Now Vandermin's challenging us as a group—as an integral part of the national defences. Above everything else, we have to be sure we've a good chance before we take counter-measures."

Elliott said with a shrug: "I suppose so. But boldness pays at times, old boy."

He couldn't have enjoyed being cautious at the chalet.

Craigie turned to Merrick.

"Jim, when Judy Ryall said that she would come in with us, do you think she knew everything involved? The risks, and—"

"She did," Merrick assured him quietly.

"Did you brief her on how to get a message through?"

"I'd made a start—with the colour powders and calling any police station."

"Don't mind me," said Elliott, "but love's a funny thing. Also pretty women in love. She could have promised to play so as to get to her hubby."

Merrick knew that; had always known it; but he wanted to shout Elliott down, to deny the very possibility. He didn't.

"I know," Craigie said, "the chance we take."

Loftus broke into the discussion for the first time for ten minutes. He was sitting on the arm of a big chair, nursing his tankard.

"We can be pretty sure that if Alec's alive, Judy'll be taken straight to him. So, get her, get Alec."

Merrick's heart began to pound.

"Do you know where she is?"

"Yes," Craigie said quietly. "She's at Arden's other house. There's no doubt, Jim. That's why we think it's likely that Alec's there. I wish you'd kept the letter from him; I could have checked the handwriting."

"She wouldn't part," Merrick said.

"It can't be helped. Now, listen, you two." Craigie stood up, and looked almost like his old self. His shoulders squared, there seemed more vigour in his pathetically thin body. "We simply have to find out whether Alec has given this information away or whether Vandermin has another source. That's priority. We're going to give them twenty-four hours to let Alec and Judy meet. By that time Judy should know the truth about Alec. We'll get her back—" he paused, and actually smiled. "We *must* get her back."

"What happens if she's taken away from this house—can we trace her, or will he fool us?" Elliott was back in his more sombre mood.

"I think we can trace her," Craigie said. "I think we've one string Arden doesn't know about."

"Corlett on the job?" Elliott asked. He didn't voice a question, yet seemed to say: "Corlett hasn't done much of a job with Arden yet."

And Corlett had lost track of Arden all along.

"No, someone else. Roy's resting. I want you to rest, too, Jim. You've probably got twenty-four hours." Craigie gave nothing of his thoughts away. But 'rested' might mean 'suspended'.

"I'm tired of taking it easy," Merrick growled, but wasn't so hopelessly depressed as he had been. Craigie knew where Judy was and wanted her back; his, Merrick's, desperate desire and the need of the Department were the same.

"Don't forget that Vandermin may have another go at you," Loftus said.

"Oh, not much need to worry about that," said Elliott, with a bright smile. "He has a low opinion of yours truly and our Jim, or he wouldn't have sent us to bye-byes and then let us wake up. For that reason alone," Elliott went on very softly, "I will gladly punch Vandermin on the nose until his middle name changes to Rudolph. Coming, Jim?"

17

ATTACK

M uscles in trim?" asked Elliott, lightly. "Eye steady, nerve strong, all that kind of thing?"

"Why don't you keep quiet sometimes?" Merrick demanded; but there was a hint of laughter in his voice.

"Congenital inability," Elliott assured him gravely. "Father says it began with mother; she was never known to stop talking, either. Still, a clever student of human nature like you ought to have discovered my guilty secret by now. The more I talk, the more nervous I am. Ever pause to think what depends on this show to-night?"

Merrick didn't answer.

It was late afternoon. They were together in Merrick's flat; they'd spent the morning there and lunched together, and they were due to separate in half an hour, then to make their different ways to a meeting place near the house where Arden was known to be.

He was still there, according to Craigie's agents on the spot; and so was Judy.

They had studied maps, including a large-scale survey map

of the district. They had gone over the road to the house so that they would be able to find their way there blindfolded. They knew what the house looked like, where the windows were, what doors were there, too. They knew what buildings were nearby, how far it was to the nearest farm and the nearest village, and what other assault arrangements had been made.

Nervous in case they were discovered, Craigie and Loftus had arranged for other agents to install two small radio transmitters on the walkie-talkie principle, near the house, which was called Red Walls. At different places nearby were stores of arms. It was planned as a military action, but in the beginning only Elliott and Merrick were to make the approach; too many would give warning.

Of the thirty odd members of the Department engaged in this, few knew exactly what was being planned. There were the two who had been watching the house for some time— unknown to Arden, it was hoped—and Elliott, Merrick. Others would be ready to be rushed to Red Walls if the need arose, but at this stage they had no idea why they had been told to find their way to St. Albans or to a little village nearby.

Nothing suggested that Arden knew that the house was under observation.

"Okay, have it your own way," Elliott said. "Don't pause to think. I'll tell you what depends on to-night's show. The future of (a) Department Z, (b) British counter-espionage for a long time to come and (c) the safe custody of a large quantity of secret information. Just on you and me, old chap; it's lucky we've broad shoulders. One odd thing."

Merrick grunted: "What?"

"If Craigie can't trace where the formulæ and whatnot goes, where does it go? What's Vandermin, if there is such a chap as Vandermin, going to do with it?"

"That's one of the things we're supposed to find out," Merrick said gruffly.

"Dear boy, don't be sour," rebuked Elliott. "Just a rhetorical question. I'm going soon and you can brood in silence." He lit a cigarette, and the match flared dangerously close to his fluffy moustache. "Ever have that nasty feeling that Gordon may be wrong again? That Arden may be expecting us?" He shivered. "I never liked being a fly."

Merrick didn't speak.

"Er—hate to be solemn," Elliott went on, "but you don't dote on Corlett, do you?"

Merrick said slowly:

"We just don't get on."

"I know what you mean," Elliott said. "I'm not surprised. I've been doing a lot of thinking about our boy with the dark Spanish eyes. He's let Arden go a sight too often. He . . ."

Merrick said quietly:

"I don't like Corlett but I've no reason to think he's a traitor. If you have, you ought to tell Craigie."

Elliott shrugged.

"I have done," he said. "And Corlett's resting. Interesting, isn't it?"

Merrick stood beneath a tree in a lane near Red Walls, looking at the outline of the house against the brightly star-lit sky. It was half-past eleven. There were two lighted windows at the house; according to their information, all lights usually went out before midnight, but this could be an exception.

A breeze lent a little crispness to the warm night air.

Elliott was due here at any time; he surely wouldn't be long. Then they would go together to a small copse nearby, where the two Department Z agents had been hiding for some time.

These two had made a kind of dug-out, and the top had

JOHN CREASEY

been covered with turf and bushes; nothing suggested that anyone suspected that they were there. They would expect Elliott and Merrick at midnight exactly.

The night was very quiet.

Merrick lit a cigarette, cupping his hand round his light carefully, making sure that no flame showed. His car was in a field, not far away; he had come along the narrow road without headlights. The house, just a low, dark mass against the sky, was isolated, except for a farmhouse half a mile or so away.

A drive led up to Red Walls.

Merrick moved about, cautiously. He wondered if Arden had guards in the grounds, and what precautions were taken at the house. In view of everything that had happened, he couldn't understand how Craigie had managed to find this place out, without betraying his men. But what mattered was that he had.

Merrick stood still, suddenly, and listened. He heard a sound, not far off; footsteps. He stood close to the trunk of the big oak. The footfalls were on turf, and his acute hearing warned him that someone was approaching.

The man drew nearer.

After a pause, Elliott called softly: "You there, Jim?"

"Aye, aye," Merrick whispered, and his heart steadied. He moved forward, and they met close to the narrow road leading to Red Wall. "All quiet."

"Fine."

"Won't be long," Merrick said.

"No. Just had a word with Loftus on the radio; he's with the troops at the village." It was easy to imagine Elliott's smile; and he would use the word 'troops' for the Z agents, a dozen of whom were with Loftus. "He says that all's well. No sign of movement from the house. He's been comparing notes with the other battalion in the village, and all's well there, too. At this moment, they're spreading out in a large cordon, and then they'll close in. By the time we start, the grounds will be completely surrounded, and Arden won't have a chance of getting anyone away."

"Good," Merrick said.

"Sound more optimistic, James!"

"Let's go and see these two johnnies," Merrick said.

"Right, sir!"

But for the desperate need for secrecy, they would have visited the dug-out before. As it was, they knew what to do, where to go, what signal to give if the Department Z men weren't there to greet them. They walked on the grass at the side of the road through the quiet night. The copse was on a hill, almost on a level with Red Walls; as good a vantage point as there could be. The drive sloped downhill from the house, and soon they could make out the white gates at the end of the drive.

The two lighted windows still showed.

"Nice to be handing it out for a change," Elliott remarked. "You'll never know how I wanted to put a bullet through Arden's head when he was running for that cable car."

"Forget it."

"Anything to oblige," Elliott said, then added softly: "Lovely, isn't she?"

Merrick didn't speak.

They left the road at a five-barred gate which, they had been told, would be open. It was. They walked uphill, concealed by the hedge which was behind them; no one looking from the house would see them. The fence which surrounded the garden of Red Walls was only fifty yards or so away. The copse where the dug-out was now less than a hundred yards away. Hidden within fairly easy reach were two jeeps.

Craigie and Loftus had used every trick they knew to make sure the odds were favourable.

And it should mean rescuing Judy . . .

They reached the fringe of the copse. No one was about. It was darker here, for the leafy branches of the trees hid most of the sky and the stars. There were the usual rustlings of the night; that was all.

"Anyone about," Elliott whispered, and then gave a stifled giggle. "Lord, no, we're owls, aren't we?" Judging from his manner, his nerves were almost at breaking point, he just couldn't keep quiet. But he gave a fair imitation of the hoot of an owl—the signal which the two men in the dug-out were expecting.

There was no answering call, and Elliott tried again. Merrick peered about the trees, hoping to see some sign of movement; there was none.

"*Too-witt—too-woo,*" Elliott called again.

There was still no answer.

"Odd," he murmured. "Think we can find the spot?" He looked down at the ground, and Merrick heard the click of a torch; but it didn't go on. "They can see flashlights at the house. Jim, this can't have gone wrong, can it?"

Merrick said: "Of course not," with more vigour than he meant. But the silence was beginning to alarm him.

"Try again."

"*Too-witt—too-whooooo.*"

"Don't overdo it, you fool!"

The sound faded away gradually, and there was no answer. Then across the fields there came a sound which travelled clearly and had a beauty all its own; the striking of the village clock. Each stroke sounded clearly, but so far away that there was no harshness.

"Witching hour," Elliott said, and his voice seemed dry and much more strained. "I don't like—"

"Look!" breathed Merrick.

He saw the body first. It was in a clearing, where the stars shone limpidly upon rough grass. The man was stretched out, with his face buried in his hands, and lying face downwards, his figure dark against the grass.

Elliott made a noise in his throat.

Merrick went forward quickly.

"Careful," breathed Elliott.

Merrick went down on one knee. Whether they were watched or not, he couldn't wait; he kept his back to the house, and flashed a torch on to the face of the man who was lying there. The mouth was open a little, so were the glazed eyes—as a man might be if he were dead of gas poisoning. His body was slack, and he didn't move.

"But only half an hour or so ago he radioed Loftus," Elliott said chokily. "Is he—dead?"

"I think so," Merrick growled. He let the man fall gently, then stood up. He looked along the clearing and then saw a mound beneath some trees, only a few yards away. He went towards it. There was a hole in the mound, and he could imagine that this man had been in there, had climbed out and crawled away to die.

Where was the other man?

What had happened?

Elliott was by his side. "There's the dug-out," he said. "Better be careful, if he were gassed there might still be plenty of the stuff about."

Merrick grunted, and pulled at some of the bushes growing on the mound; a piece of turf came away; soon, a large hole was cleared and they could see the dugout, and the other man sitting against the wall, quite still.

Elliott said: "We mustn't stay here." His voice was very sharp. "They're probably watching, they'll get us next."

Merrick didn't answer, but lowered himself into the dugout, lifted the other man, and hoisted him up into the open air. Elliott helped, but was protesting.

"Mustn't let them get us too, Jim."

"Let's use the radio," Merrick said. He was familiar with the walkie-talkie, and in the dug-out he could safely shine his torch without risk of being seen from the house. He switched on. "Hallo, there, Merrick calling Loftus, Merrick calling Loftus."

"Just a minute," a man said, "just a minute." There was a pause. Then: "Hallo," came Loftus's voice. "All well with you, Jim?"

"No. The two fellows here are gassed. I think they've had it."

Loftus breathed: *"No!"*

Merrick didn't speak. Elliott was crouching at the top of the dug-out, but every now and again he turned and looked away, as if to make sure that they weren't being followed.

Loftus said: "Anything—else?"

"Two lights are still on at the house. I'm going up to it, and I'll try to break in. I know they'll probably have a few tricks up their sleeve but they might fall for the Arden method." Merrick put emphasis on the 'I'm' to try to tell Loftus he wasn't committing Elliott. "Okay?"

Loftus said: "Jim, I don't think you'll have a chance. If they've located our two—"

"I'm going," Merrick said abruptly. "Close in as soon as you can, and that'll give me a chance." He switched off, put the radio down, then clambered out of the dugout. Elliott was standing and watching the big house; and there were still two lighted windows. "Did you hear?" asked Merrick.

"Yes."

"Coming?"

"Try to keep me away," Elliott said in a high-pitched voice. "Just try to keep me away."

18

RED WALLS

They reached the fence which bordered the garden of the house. It was made of three strands of wire, and easy enough to climb, but they stood and looked at it before Elliott took a tiny piece of wire from his pocket, and let it fall on the fence. Nothing happened; there was no flash.

"Not live," he said.

"No," said Merrick. Those two lighted windows seemed to beckon him, and he vaulted the wire. Elliott followed, and they walked across meadowland towards the first lawns and the flower beds in front of the house.

No one appeared.

No one seemed to be patrolling the fence. No one shouted out or challenged them. No shot came out of the quiet night. A long way off, car engines started up, and Merrick knew that Loftus and his 'troops' were on their way. Loftus had realised that ten minutes might make a difference, that was why he hadn't ordered them to wait for him.

"Place seems—deserted," Elliott muttered.

"Yes." Merrick's mind was working more swiftly now, and

clearly. Half an hour ago, the two men who were now gassed, probably dead, had reported that no one had left the house. He had been watching it for at least half an hour, and had seen no one leave.

That didn't add up.

He puzzled over it as they reached the front door. He didn't know what to expect. He wasn't sure that they would live to see the night out; or for that matter, live through the next hour. But the silence was uncanny. How could people have left, without being seen?

Had they left?

"What do we do?" asked Elliott. "The Arden touch—just knock and ring?"

Merrick said: "I don't know whether—" and then stopped. There was a light on in the hall, he could see now, and the front door was open; a crack of light showed at one side. He pushed it. It opened wider, swinging back silently. Yet the silence seemed filled with laughter, the sneering laughter of Joshua Arden.

"They've—flown," Elliott said in a hollow voice. "Blow me down! They wouldn't have left the door open, would they? I think—"

Merrick stepped inside. It was a spacious hall, with panelled walls, two big tapestries and some oil paintings hanging, and antique furniture; there was an atmosphere of good taste as well as of wealth. A brightly-lit chandelier stood above their heads, absolutely still although the colours showed boldly in the glass.

". . . we ought to wait for Loftus," Elliott said.

"You wait," said Merrick. "I'm going to find out whether they've been here."

He hurried forward.

Elliott followed him.

They went into the four rooms downstairs, and found each empty. There were traces suggesting that the house had been occupied that evening. Ash-trays with cigarette-ends—two had lipstick on—and several empty glasses with whisky, gin and syphons of soda, were in a big lounge furnished in gold and blue. One of the glasses had lipstick on the rim, too.

Neither man spoke.

The kitchen quarters were deserted. Everything there was modern and spick-and-span, and cooking was done by electricity. The lights were on, and one of the hotplates seemed warm.

"Where are the villains?" breathed Elliott. "That's the boiling question!" He sounded as if he had a frog in his throat. "There's been a woman of sorts here. Jim, believe it or not I'm not a coward by nature, but I do not like this establishment. I've a nasty feeling that it might suddenly blow up and take me with it! If you know what I mean."

"You look for a cellar and see if you can find anything," Merrick said. "I'm going to try the bedrooms." They were back in the hall, close to the stairs. He hurried up, footsteps muffled by the thick carpet, hand at his pocket holding his gun. But at heart he knew that the gun wouldn't serve any purpose here. This house was empty; if there were danger, then it would come in the way that Elliott half-feared. Yet he wasn't frightened physically. There were those traces of lipstick; it might be Judy's. It would be something to prove that she was still alive; or to have reason for thinking that she was.

Two passages led off the landing.

Merrick turned right. There were doors on either side, each of them ajar. One light was on. He looked in that room first, but it was empty. There were signs of hurried departure— the only sign of this that he found everywhere. Drawers weren't pushed back into position, and a few oddments of men's clothes were on a bed.

He went into the next room—and knew at once that Judy had been in here. It was hard to say why, at first, but he was sure of it. He looked round quickly, and found traces of powder, a few bright hair grips of the kind she used; a dozen little indications. There were no clothes, but then her clothes had been packed in the case taken from the airport, and there was no reason why she should have packed again.

He went into two other rooms, but found nothing of interest, then went along to the other passage. Here were two large rooms, luxuriously furnished and with bathrooms attached. He found a bloodstained bandage in one bathroom, and first aid oddments which suggested that a wound had been dressed here recently; so this was Arden's. He didn't spend much time there, but hurried into the next room.

This was different.

The mahogany wardrobe had two suits in it; there were several pairs of shoes, shirts, everything one would expect to find in a man's room. And there was a pipe—

Merrick looked at it, and caught his breath. It was small and almost red; Alec's pipe. It was a pipe almost by courtesy, contrasting it with Gordon Craigie's meerschaum made it look ludicrous—but there it was, the silly little pipe which Alec Ryall had smoked for years.

Merrick picked it up.

He turned, and saw several other things which were undoubtedly Alec's; a cigarette-case, a little leather case for book-matches. They were at a desk in front of the window, where heavy curtains were drawn.

Merrick turned away, slowly.

He went across to the wardrobe, and took out two pairs of shoes, picked them up and examined them. The Department taught one to observe the 'little' things, of the kind that could make or break a man. Alec always walked slightly inwards, not enough to notice but enough to wear the soles of his shoes a little beneath the spot where the big toe would be.

These were worn that way.

There were three pairs; black, brown and brogue; and they were Alec's size.

The room had a lived-in look, smelt faintly of tobacco, and looked as if Alec were expected back at any moment. Everything gave the impression that everyone here had just got up and walked out—not to leave the house, but to go from one room to another.

They hadn't been seen to leave, remember.

Merrick went carefully through everything, shifting item by item—and then he touched a cigarette-case, slim, gold. He thought he recognised it.

He picked it up and studied the initials; R.C. for Roy Corlett; he knew that it was Corlett's.

And Corlett was 'resting'!

Merrick turned out of this room. There was an attic, but the hatch door was bolted on the inside, and there was no chance of anyone coming out that way. He ran down the stairs, calling:

"Ted!"

Elliott didn't answer.

Merrick went along to the kitchen. There was a washhouse leading off that, and a door leading to a cellar leading off the wash-house.

"Ted!"

Still no one answered—but outside the sounds of engines came clear, and probably Loftus and the 'troops' were halfway up the drive. Merrick ran into the wash-house, and saw that the door leading to the cellar was ajar; a light shone beyond it. His discovery seemed to burn into him.

"Ted," he called, and opened the door—and then drew back sharply.

He didn't waste much time, but jolted himself into action and hurried down the wooden steps. Elliott was half-way down, crawling up them. There was blood on his forehead, more streaking down his cheek, congealing on his moustache.

He said something which Merrick didn't hear as he clattered down the stairs. They were a very long, steep flight.

Elliott waved at him, as if sending him away. The man's grey eyes were wide open, rounded—fearful!

"Get away—tell the others!" His voice came more clearly now, and he waved at Merrick again. "Blowing—up!"

Merrick was almost in front of him. Footsteps sounded above their heads; Loftus and the others were in the house. And Elliott wouldn't talk and behave like this unless he were sure that disaster was close.

Merrick bellowed: "Get away, going to blow up!" and bent down and raised Elliott to his knees. "Careful," he said, without really knowing what he was saying. He hoisted the other high, managed to get him over his shoulder. *"Blow up coming!"* he roared, and then saw a shadowy figure appear at the doorway, cast by the washroom light. Was it Loftus? *"Get away, blow up coming!"*

The shadow disappeared; but another appeared, and turned into a man who came clattering down. It was Bob Kerr.

"Help you," he said, as calmly as if he were asking for a light. He took Elliott's feet, and Merrick held on to his shoulders; between them, they carried Elliott up to the wash-house, face downwards.

Loftus was there, issuing instructions calmly.

"Papers from study, Tim—search the library, Joe—Dick,

have a look round the bedrooms, I'll come with you. The rest—
out. Stay near enough to pick up the pieces. Hallo, Jim, you still
with us?"

They were putting Elliott down carefully. Blood dripped
from his forehead to the floor, and he winced when one of
them touched his left foot. But he could speak in a much
clearer voice.

"Place will blow up, Bill. Don't think I heard the tick-tock
ticking downstairs. Nothing so simple—caught a man lighting
a fuse. Tried to put it out, but slipped." He forced a grin, and
wiped his moustache, smearing the blood more. "Must get
away, old boy. Prefer to be buried all in one piece."

"Yes—get him outside," Loftus said to two men who were
standing by. "And you go, Jim."

"I'm coming with you," Merrick said sharply.

"Get the hell out of here when I say so!" roared Loftus. His
voice echoed about the room, for a split second he looked
furious enough to strike Merrick. Just then, if he hadn't
before, Merrick understood what Loftus was feeling; and the
training of years taught him to do exactly what he was told.

"Okay. Sorry."

"Be with you soon," Loftus said, quiet in a moment. "We'll
chuck anything we find out of the windows, don't go too far.
Hurry, chaps."

Those who were on duty in the house stayed; the others,
Merrick among them, went out. The night seemed colder.
There were half a dozen cars, all with their headlights on, all
turned towards the house; the blaze of light made it possible
to see the grounds, the flowers, the house and the men in
clearest detail.

But the house might—would—blow up.

Loftus was in there, going through the rooms for papers
which he would probably never find; which probably weren't

there, anyhow. Arden wouldn't have left any papers behind; he would know there was a risk that the place would be searched before it was destroyed.

Merrick felt a gripping tension; fear for Loftus was one cause, but there was more. Judy had been in this house, and there was little doubt that Alec had, too. Little doubt? He couldn't see any at all. There were Alec's clothes, that pipe, shoes the way Alec wore his, the other oddments; and all in a room as luxurious as Arden's, which didn't suggest that he was much of a prisoner.

A 'kind of prisoner' he'd said.

And there was Corlett.

Elliott was lifted into a car, and men were bending over him.

"Only a sprained ankle," one said. "He won't have much of a scar on his face, either. Don't wake him, do him good to be under the weather for a bit. Must have felt like hell."

"Don't you?" asked another.

Merrick heard but hardly noticed what they said. He turned and watched the house, saw the figures moving inside the rooms, dreaded the moment when the explosion would come. Why didn't Loftus hurry?

How had Arden got away?

That was the trouble, he could never concentrate on one thing at a time, it was impossible to be sure what was the most important. Was it? How had Arden got away, where was he, where had he taken Judy and Alec?

The steep flight of stairs, which went so far down—stairs leading to what? Just to a cellar? Or to a tunnel? A subterranean tunnel, why not? What was the matter with his mind, of course that was it. And where would they come out? Of a hole in the ground, like the dug-out, or in another building? Corlett had probably told them about the two men watching them, so they'd probably guessed how closely the surrounding district was being guarded. They'd want cover somewhere, and the only building nearby was the farmhouse down in the valley.

The house still stood in that blaze of light.

Loftus was throwing something out of the window.

Merrick called: "Anyone without a job, this way." He ran towards one of the cars and took the wheel—and before he started the engine, three men were with him, others were hurrying. "Just a hunch," he said tautly. "But there was a tunnel, it could lead to the farmhouse. We're going to find out. Two car loads, the more the merrier."

One man was climbing in beside him already, others were getting into the back. Four more ran to a jeep and clambered into it. Engines roared.

The house still stood, and the figures were at the windows. Merrick switched on the headlights as he turned the car on the lawn, and the light shone on the nodding heads, of summer flowers, seeming to rob them of colour. He glanced round at the house, and saw a man climbing out of a window.

He trod on the accelerator.

The car shot forward. He sensed that the others were turning and looking at the house. He could hardly think, just gritted his teeth and kept going—because Arden might be in that farmhouse, with Judy, with Alec.

Behind him, a man said tensely:

"Up she goes."

Then Merrick saw the flash . . .

19

THE FARMHOUSE

The flash would have blinded Merrick had he been looking straight on to it. It lit up the sky. It showed the trees and the hedges, the valley and the fields, the distant hills. It was like a tremendous flash of sheet lightning as it flickered for a split second; then abysmal blackness seemed to descend upon them.

Merrick took his foot off the accelerator and jammed on the brake, momentarily out of control, waiting for something which didn't come—but which he knew wasn't far away. The 'thunder'.

It came.

It seemed to split the night; as if Jove had come down from the heavens and was rampaging the fields. It boomed and roared and reverberated about their ears, deafening; far worse than the blinding flash.

After that came the blast.

Merrick wasn't ready for it. The wheel was wrenched out of his hand; he knew that the car was being blown to one side, felt himself falling, banged his head against the roof. Suddenly the car righted itself. Merrick was jolted out of his seat against the man sitting beside him; and the engine stalled. There was a strange sighing sound, going further and further away as the blast travelled across the fields and valleys.

Merrick sat quite still.

He heard a different sound, as of a man speaking close to his ear in a hoarse voice. He turned his head. Yes, the Department Z man next to him was saying something, but it couldn't really matter. Then the man looked behind him, and Merrick did the same.

The house, or what was left of it, was a burning mass. Flames were leaping high into the sky, and a lurid red glow spread everywhere.

"We can't do a thing," the man next to him said hoarsely. "Better get on. Get on."

No, they couldn't do a thing.

Loftus might have been in the house, and some of the others, too. They had been warned but had preferred to take a chance because there might be papers which would help them to trace Vandermin. Craigie could open his little black book again to-morrow, and make more entries; like notches in a gun for the friends one had killed.

The firelight leapt behind them, and a red glow danced on the instrument panel and the windscreen. Merrick started the engine again savagely. No one in the car spoke, and Merrick didn't see the other car. Had it withstood the blast? Had anyone, except them? Certainly no one who had been inside the house could have had a chance. Loftus—

Forget Loftus—get to the farmhouse.

There was no light but that of the fire behind them; the jeep wasn't following. So it had been damaged, and the men in it might have been killed by that blast; they'd been much nearer than he.

Well, there were four of them.

They drove into the red-tinged night, passed through the open drive gates, and turned right towards the farmhouse. He knew exactly where it was; his mind was almost a relief map of the district. And they could see because of the blazing house; but that would soon die down.

The man by his side said something.

"What's that?" His own voice was hoarse, and he knew that it didn't travel far.

"Gun?"

"What gun?"

"Have you a gun?"

"Yes, why?"

"Might need it."

'Idiot,' thought Merrick and then caught a glimpse of the man grinning. They were crazy, they were impossible. There was Elliott, imploring them to get out of the house, yet saying that he wanted to be buried all in one piece. Nothing could kill their flippancy. But in them as in him there was a savage hatred for Corlett, for all the men responsible for these things. Next to Craigie, Loftus was each man's hero.

"How much further?"

"What?"

"How far now?"

"'Bout a mile."

"Sure?"

"Yes."

"Well, don't go to sleep, we want to get there to-night."

Lunatic.

They came to a sharp bend in the road, where there were trees on either side; a nasty blind turning. Merrick slowed down a fraction, and took it on two wheels. He felt the other man lean against him and heard the tyres screeching. It didn't matter. The car straightened itself, and they were travelling along the narrow road at sixty miles an hour, when the man by his side shouted:

"Look there!"

This time it wasn't for the sake of hearing his own voice. There were car headlamps not far away; three sets and behind the cars was the shape of the farmhouse. It would have been invisible but for the light from the burning house behind them, as it was it was just a dark blotch. But the cars were there, speeding along this road.

"Must stop the devils." That was the man by his side, almost as garrulous as Elliott.

"Shut up." Merrick looked at the relief map photographed inside his mind. The farmhouse had a short private road, which led into this—was simply a continuation of this. There were cross-roads between here and the farm. To get to St. Albans the people in the other cars would have to turn right; the other road led across country. It was impossible to judge how far the distant cars were from the cross-roads. The beams of their headlights shone out, showing hedges and telegraph poles.

Merrick put his foot down. The car roared along at eighty, scraping hedges on either side. He sensed that the others had their guns out, were ready for battle; but he wasn't thinking of battle, he was thinking that Judy was there. Judy, Alec, Arden, Corlett. If a car were overturned, going at that speed, there wouldn't be much chance for the passengers. He didn't want to shoot.

They were near enough.

They reached the last stretch before the cross-roads, and the first of the other cars swung to the right. At the same moment, the men behind Merrick started shooting through the windows. There wasn't a thing he could do to stop them;

couldn't be sure that he ought even to try. Didn't they know everything they wanted now?

What was Judy thinking, now that she knew Alec was—

Forget Judy, Alec, everything; get those cars!

The shooting was loud in his ears, and there was an acrid, biting smell of cordite. The first car had turned the corner and was now hurtling towards St. Albans. The second reached the corner—and then Merrick heard an explosion, guessed that a tyre had burst, and saw the car slew over to one side.

It seemed to leap into the air, then turn turtle. He heard it crash. He felt the blood drain from his cheeks, in dread that Judy was in that car; but there was no time to do anything.

The leading car was a long way off now, they couldn't catch up with it; but the third couldn't pass the wreck at speed, might not be able to pass it at all.

It turned right.

The second car might catch fire, too. This was a night for fire.

Merrick prayed.

Then he heard different sounds; the others were shooting at him, at this car. The sound was the metallic pinging of bullets on the wings. He could see that the driver of the third car from the farmhouse was trying to squeeze between the hedge and the wreckage.

The man by Merrick's side opened his door and jumped out—then gave a little coughing noise, and fell.

The third car got passed the obstacle and shot after the first. There was only the middle car to worry about now, and if Judy had been in there—

Merrick got out.

One of the other men was bending over the wounded Department agent. The second went with Merrick towards the smash.

One man had been flung clear, and was lying in an odd position by the side of the road. There was a strong smell of petrol—and fear in Merrick that the fire might start after all. He drew nearer, heart pounding; until he had known Judy, he had never known it pound so fiercely.

He couldn't see in spite of the headlamps behind him. He shone his torch into the wreckage of the crashed car. Inside was another man whom he didn't recognise; and a woman.

Merrick shone the torch through the window, and light fell upon the woman's skirt and on her legs; but he could not see her face. The great fear in him seemed to drain the blood out of his body. He couldn't find words. The stench of petrol seemed to grow stronger, and he wondered if there were still time for the car to blow up. A long way off, the headlights of the two cars which had escaped were white against the night; but he didn't look towards them, couldn't think about anything else but the woman here.

Judy?

How could he get in, and find out? How could he open the window, the door? All were jammed. He pushed and pulled at both; nothing happened. There was the woman, huddled in the corner, and—there was blood. It came dripping from beneath her hat. Drip—drip—drip—bright red, on to the side of the car.

"Need a break-down van," his companion said.

"What?"

"Break-down van."

"Oh, yes." Merrick hardly knew what the other said or what he himself was saying. He went down first on his knees and then flat on his stomach, and shone the torch through the back window; then he saw that this window was smashed and that he could get an arm through and perhaps reach the crouching woman.

A KIND OF PRISONER

She was dead, of course; her body was hopelessly crushed.

He grunted as he laid the torch down so that it shone into the car, and then stretched his right arm inside. It wasn't easy. His fingers were inches away from the woman when he felt his shoulder come up against the window frame. He edged his way a little further. The torchlight shone on a pool of blood, which was dripping from the unseen head. All he needed to see was the hair; if it were auburn, it was Judy.

Who else would it be?

He grunted again as he managed to get his arm further into the car; then he touched the hat with his fingers. Slowly, agonisingly because of the strain at his shoulder, he moved the hat to one side. It moved very slowly; it was just resting on his finger tips, and it might fall, he would have to begin it all over again.

Then he saw the woman's hair—*fair* hair, golden-hued.

So it wasn't Judy.

Relief swept over him, and made him relax. He drew his hand back a little and the hat fell into place again. That didn't matter. He lay there for several seconds, then heard the sound of a car engine, followed by the voice of his companion.

"Others coming—you all right?"

"Yes," Merrick grunted. He withdrew his arm, stood up, and rubbed his shoulder slowly. "Yes." It wasn't Judy, and in spite of everything else that had happened he couldn't think beyond that, didn't even worry about the approaching car or who was in it.

What an agent!

Where was Judy now?

Who was coming?

20

EYES FROM THE SKY

W ell, what's doing here?" a man asked.
For the first time that night Merrick really put
Judy out of his mind for a moment—because the voice
brought shock with it, and relief.

It was Loftus.

"Oh, just a road-hog," said Merrick's companion. "You
ought to have Merrick's licence withdrawn, he's not safe."
There was a pause. "Small fry, I'm afraid, the big chaps got
away. One woman in here, with a man I don't know. Chap
thrown out."

Loftus, massive in the headlights, said sharply to Merrick.

"Judy?"

"No—fair-haired."

"Oh," said Loftus, "that's something." Now Merrick could
see that his hair was singed, his right eyebrow seemed to have
disappeared altogether, and there were one or two nasty
looking burn marks on his cheek. But he was completely
himself, casual and commanding. "So you smoked 'em out,

162

Jim. Bad luck you didn't have five minutes more to play with. Nearest we've got to them when we've really meant business—and we mean business. How many cars got away?"

"Two."

"Oh, well," Loftus said, "we can still hope." He glanced up at the starlit sky, so peaceful here, and there was a faint sound of an aeroplane engine. He didn't go on, but looked towards the farmhouse, which was in complete darkness.

"What's on your mind?"

"I think I know what's caused most of our trouble," Merrick said. "I found Corlett's cigarette-case at Red Walls."

After a long pause, Loftus said softly:

"Did you then. Gordon and I—"

"Bill!" called an agent abruptly. "Come here!"

He was bending over the man who had been thrown from the car. Loftus and Merrick joined him—and looked down on Corlett's face, his handsome eyes closed in death.

They said little, made sure that Corlett was dead, and then moved away from the body.

"I hope they haven't laid on an explosion here, too," Loftus said. "I'd better go and see. You stay here, Jim."

"That's right," Merrick said, and turned and walked by Loftus's side. Loftus looked at him sharply, then smiled faintly, that was quite visible in the headlights of the cars which were turned towards them. "Okay, Jim," he said. "I'm glad it's not Judy. Could be Iris Arden."

"I—suppose so."

"Fair hair," mused Loftus. "We'll soon see. Did you find that bedroom of Alec's?"

"Yes."

"The trouble about that," said Loftus, in a far away voice, "is that Alec knew more about the Department than anyone else, except Gordon and me. Much more than Corlett. Alec was coming along for the third in command. God knows how they managed to break him down—but obviously they have. It means building up again almost from nothing; we now know that we can't use anything that we've used before. Arden called up to tell us he'd got Judy," Loftus added, in that calm, casual but somehow unreal voice, "and spelt his name backwards."

Merrick gulped.

"And as Vandermin knows so much, we just have to find him and smash them up," Loftus said, and added as if wryly: "If it's the last thing we do. They know too much. From now on, a matter of life or death, as they say?"

But he couldn't really make himself sound flippant.

"What hope is there of finding them?" Merrick demanded; and he asked because of what Loftus had said, not because of Judy.

"Fair. Had helicopters out. Vandermin doesn't know everything and he hasn't got Corlett any more," Loftus went on. "We've been so cautious in case it was someone other than Alec giving the dope away that we've been very cagey. So no one except Gordon and I knew until now. Three helicopters. They'd spot those cars, see the crash, and be after the other two. Who said we couldn't live on hope?" They were actually in the farmhouse yard. "Place hasn't blown up yet, anyhow. Trouble is," he added, standing quite still and looking down at Merrick, "we're hunting for Alec Ryall now. He's more deadly than any of them. Hell of a job. I wonder which way Judy will turn."

"Our way."

"Love's a funny thing," Loftus said cryptically.

Dawn, with a lovely red-tinged glow, crept across the eastern sky and shone upon the farmhouse with its timbered walls and the squat red chimney and lichen-covered red tiles.

It shone upon the byres and the sheds and the fowls which scratched among the straw and dirt of the yard; on the milkmen coming from their cottages, some way off, to profess surprise and innocence, which was probably quite true. The sun shone on the trim lawns and the old-fashioned flower garden, crammed with perennials; on the cars; on the wreckage which had already been pulled to one side, to allow traffic to pass to and fro.

The dead woman was Iris Arden.

Arden hadn't been with her, only Corlett and a man—also dead—who was unknown to Loftus.

Nothing useful had been found at the farmhouse.

Loftus had found a few papers at the big house, but was not optimistic about them. He wasn't relieved because they knew about Corlett and had nothing more to fear from his betrayals.

By the time dawn was upon them, Merrick knew that three men had been killed in the explosion and the fire, and that Loftus had been saved because he had been standing by the front door, been blown into the night, and sheltered in a small sunken garden. Several other lives had been saved in the same way.

Loftus was at the wheel of a car, Merrick by his side, two other Department agents were behind them. Loftus drove slowly, as if determined to take no chances. No one spoke; all were tired out, their faces drawn, as much because of the memory of what had happened as from the lack of sleep. They passed through St. Albans, and Loftus stopped at a roadside police patrol, had a word with the man in charge, then took the wheel again.

"No messages," he said.

"When shall we know?" asked Merrick.

"Depends when they run to earth," Loftus said. "There's always the danger that they've fled the country."

Merrick didn't speak.

There was Judy, back with her Alec, knowing the truth now and facing her own battle. There was the desperate need to smash Vandermin and his whole gang, but little prospect of doing it, as far as Merrick could see. They'd had their chance. If they'd worked a little earlier the night before, not waited until midnight, there might have been a different tale to tell. As it was, Arden and the others had been warned in time to make use of the tunnel which, it was now proved, led from Red Walls to the farmhouse.

The farmer and his wife, sole occupants as far as the neighbours knew, had also gone. That was another angle to work; there were always new angles to work, but what was the good of believing that they would be able to defeat a man who could anticipate every move they made?

Merrick found himself dozing; but there was the weight of depression, almost of despair, in him. A friend turned traitor; a woman so desperately in love now torn between loyalty and that love; a Department which was his hero, the hero of every agent, in grave danger of its very life. Gordon Craigie, looking as if he were heading for the grave; and hope pinned on helicopters!

They reached London about seven o'clock, and went straight to the office. Craigie was there, looking exactly as when Merrick had last seen him; it was hard to believe that he had slept since.

His eyes were as bright as ever.

"I've just had news," he said. "The two cars parted company on the other side of Watford, but as we had two helicopters after them, it is all right. There's a chance that they may have been mixed up with other cars, of course, but not likely. The pilots took a special night film, it's being developed now and will be round during the morning. As soon as we can, we'll pin-point the place or places. Still a hope," he added, and to Merrick's surprise, he gave a quick, almost a cheerful grin. "I'm more optimistic than I've been for a long time."

"Why?" Loftus demanded sharply.

"Herrington expects results hourly," Craigie said. "And Corlett obviously helped Arden to get away with a lot."

Herrington had been mentioned before, but Merrick didn't know him. Merrick didn't care a damn about anything but the possibility that Judy would be traced.

"So Corlett's been selling out," Craigie went on, in the same calm manner. "I suppose it was fairly obvious all the time. Another thing's worth thinking about, Bill." His voice had a confidence that was quite new; it gave Merrick new hope, too. "We've smoked them out of Red Walls and the farmhouse; that's the third place we've closed up to them. They're probably stretched out pretty thin, too. A big effort now and we'll get 'em."

Loftus didn't ask his question again.

Merrick wondered what the explanation was.

"Now, Jim, you'll want to be in the next round," Craigie said to him, as if to a child, "so you'd better get some sleep."

"Did you suspect Corlett?" Merrick asked. "And if you did, what did you do about it?"

Craigie said quietly: "We'd wondered. And we've tried to check everyone—even you." He didn't smile. "It's not so easy to screen a man with another who might need screening even more. Now we're going back over Corlett's past, screening all the agents who've worked with him—doing all we can."

Merrick had to leave it at that.

The house in Moor Street was very quiet. There was little noise in the street itself, it was always a backwater. The door

JOHN CREASEY

of the tall, handsome Mrs. Gilmour remained closed, and
Merrick found himself skipping past it quickly, then grinning
faintly almost sheepishly.

The grin faded.

He was dog tired, and it was from nervousness as well as
physical exhaustion. It wouldn't be long before he would
know for certain whether he would be able to rescue Judy, but
by far the worst possibility was that Judy might not want to be
rescued; she might prefer to stay with Alec, whatever he had
done.

"Love's a funny thing," Loftus had said solemnly.

It could change a man, turn him inside out, leave his
emotions as bare as the nerve of an aching tooth. It could turn
a young man into an ancient, make him feel as if he would
never be young again; and it could also make him feel as if he
had the secret of eternal youth, as Merrick had felt sometimes
in Switzerland.

He was at his landing, when a door below opened, footsteps came quickly and briskly on the stairs, and his heart
dropped. It dropped further when he saw Mrs. Gilmour, with
her bottle green, tight-fitting suit, her sleek black hair and
wide centre parting and bold looks.

"Oh, Mr. Merrick!"

"Why, hallo." He supposed he owed her some kind of an
explanation; a lying one, of course, but why should he have to
lie now? He needed rest even if he couldn't get to sleep. "I've
had a roughish night, and—"

"I won't keep you a moment," she said. "I had a telephone
message from a friend of yours."

"From—" he stiffened, and his tongue wouldn't work; from
Judy, who else, from Judy! "Oh," he said lamely, and hoped that
she wouldn't begin to guess that he felt as if a great dynamo
had suddenly started to work within him.

168

"A Mr. Elliott," she said, and came up to the landing, looking into his eyes. She handed him a slip of paper. "Yes, you do look tired. Is there anything I can do to help?"

"No, thanks. Very nice of you." He glanced down at the slip of paper. The writing was bold, black, with upright letters; a hand no one could ever mistake. The message read:

Mr. Elliott telephoned me, saying that he had tried the flat upstairs unsuccessfully. His ankle is responding to treatment, he will be about again during the day. Before you go out will you please telephone him at Mayfair 59561.

Merrick read it, and forced a smile.

"Thanks very much, you're very kind." He fumbled for his key. He had a feeling that Mrs. Gilmour would like to take it from his fingers and open the door for him. He wished he knew why it was that he felt self-conscious while she looked at him as she did now, with those bold, hawklike eyes. Handsome woman, but—

"Be seeing you," he said.

"If I can help, please let me know."

"I will," said Merrick, and was proud of the smile he managed to show; less proud of the fact that he pushed the door too hard; it must have seemed that he had deliberately slammed it in her face. Well, he hadn't. She had always been interested in him, and the affair in the flat and the street had given her an excuse to probe, to ask questions.

She worried him.

He lit a cigarette, but was in bed before it was half-smoked, coat, shoes and collar and tie off, the rest on. Craigie or Loftus would call him when it was time to wake up. It was an odd thing that he was able to sleep—he knew that he would be able to, of course; couldn't miss. He stubbed out the cigarette. Craigie or Loftus—what had made Craigie sound so much more confident? Something had happened during the night—

something Loftus hadn't known about when they had reached the Department office.

Merrick dozed.

Craigie did feel more cheerful, that was the main thing. And he, James Merrick, was too tired, too exhausted, to worry about anything else, even Judy. But how lovely she was; and how precious. He had told her that he was sure that if it were a choice between loyalty to her country and Alec, she would choose loyalty, but was he right? Would she? Love was a funny thing! This was a funny business. No less than a challenge on the part of Vandermin and Arden, one that would give everyone a surprise, to the Department, to British counter-espionage. Come to think, that was a pretty big lump to bite off and chew.

Craigie thought that Vandermin's resources might by now be stretched pretty thin. Well, why not? Craigie didn't guess. Craigie either knew or didn't know.

Judy . . .

Alec; Alec's pipe, Alec's shoes.

Judy.

Merrick went to sleep.

He did not know it, but he slept four hours all but three minutes, and it was five minutes to twelve when he heard a sound. At first it was hardly conscious hearing, just something stirring deep down in his sub-conscious; but gradually as his mind came to the surface, the sound did, too. A bell. Who was ringing what, where? A bell. *Brrr—brrrr: brrrr—brrrr.* Bell, blast the bell, blasted bell wouldn't stop—

Telephone bell!

He stretched out a hand and struggled up at the same time. He banged his head on the wooden head panel, but it didn't hurt; if anything it helped to clear his mind. He grabbed the receiver and put it to his ear. This would be Craigie, of course, or Loftus, with news about the photographs which the helicopter pilots had taken.

"Hallo." That was a bit hoarse. "Sorry. Hallo, this is Jim Merrick."

"Hallo, Jim," said Judy Ryall.

21
MESSAGE

M errick had never had to make a greater effort to keep his voice steady. He paused for a fraction of a second, and actually started to speak, but made no sound; then he tried again. The words came easily enough.

"Hallo, Judy."

"I told you I'd get in touch with you," she said.

"Yes, you did. Did you find Alec?" Idiot question; but at least it gave him a little time to think. Thoughts flashed into his mind—the first and most obvious, that she had been allowed to telephone him, was still under Arden's control. She had spoken the moment he had lifted the receiver, so she was somewhere in the automatic exchange area. Had the helicopters traced the cars to London? Craigie hadn't said so.

"Yes," Judy said. Merrick imagined that there was an edge to her voice—as if she were forcing herself to speak. "Yes, he's here, in the same house. You—you were right, Jim."

"I was afraid so," Merrick said. The fact that she could talk so calmly was a help. Keep rational. "How is he?"

"Oh, he's all right now. I'm going to stay with him."

"Oh," Merrick said.

"Alec has thought it out and decided that this is the right thing to do," Judy went on, very earnestly. Merrick could imagine that she was saying exactly what she had been told to say.

"I see. Where are you now?" That was his first attempt at a trick question; a poor one, but at least Merrick was beginning to tick again.

"I don't know," Judy said, "and I couldn't tell you if I did. Mr. Arden is in the room with me. Jim, I've a message for you."

Merrick said: "From Arden?"

"Yes. I wish I knew how to make you understand exactly what he means," said Judy, and the note of strain was more noticeable in her voice. "It wasn't until the last minute that he discovered about the men watching Red Walls, and he didn't like having to get out in a hurry. He—Jim, please believe me— he says that he'll kill Craigie, Loftus and every agent he can locate if you keep this up." The significance, the monstrousness of that, came home to Merrick when she paused; but she soon went on again, and he was sure that there was a note of desperation in her voice. "He means it, Jim. He says that he's already found a way of making Craigie very sick, but that was only a warning. If you keep up the hunt, he'll kill everyone he knows."

"Ah," said Merrick. He began to react vigorously against the threat, as any Department Z man would. "Nice chap, our Joshua. Why is he so spiteful? He—"

"Merrick, it's time you understood that this is serious," said Arden. His voice was matter-of-fact, his manner held the familiar touch of arrogance. "There's no time for silly persiflage, either. You will all be withdrawn or I shall wipe you out."

"Not Vandermin?"

"My leader approves," Arden said.

"Josh," said Merrick earnestly, "I'm sorry that things went as they did. I know you must feel like hell because of your wife, but that was your own fault. You won't get things all your own way. You're on the way out. Don't make any mistake about that."

Arden said clearly, expressionlessly: "Either you withdraw from this particular chase, Merrick, or you will be killed. That is a personal message and it also applies to Craigie, Loftus and the rest of your friends. We are quite serious, and we can do it."

There was a pause; then:

"Jim," said Judy, "I'm afraid he can."

The line went dead.

It wasn't a thing to telephone about; and it wasn't a thing to sit on. Merrick dialled the Whitehall number, but was answered by a stranger; he knew immediately that no one was in the office, that this man was only taking messages.

"Neither of the big boys there?" he asked.

"No, sir, but they shouldn't be long," the man answered. "Can I give them a message?"

"I'll call again, thanks." Merrick rang off, went into the kitchen and put a kettle on, made some toast, ate and drank, then called the Whitehall office again; Loftus and Craigie were still out. He didn't like that; it was an almost invariable rule for one or the other to be at the office; and if neither could be, they always arranged for another agent—Alec had often taken over. What could have taken them both away when urgent messages might be on the way?

Had they gone willingly?

He couldn't get all that Arden had said out of his mind. That threat to kill had been meant; perhaps he had killed already. The strength of Arden, of Vandermin, was double-edged. There were the men, the gangs; and there was the psychological edge, the ability to spread fear in the minds of men who seldom felt fear.

Craigie knew it.

So did Loftus.

Merrick telephoned a house in Chelsea, actually a hostel for Department Z agents, run for the Department in the same way as the Home. The housekeeper, a Mrs. Davidson, answered him. She was the widow of one of Craigie's men.

"No," she said. "They're all out." Merrick fancied that she sounded worried. "Usually one or two of them stay behind, but this time everyone's left. They hadn't been back long, after the night job."

"Any idea where they've gone?"

"They had a message from Mr. Loftus, and left at once— about an hour ago."

"Oh," said Merrick. "I see. Thanks." He felt as if he were being suffocated.

"Mr. Merrick, everything's all right, isn't it?"

"I don't know," Merrick said. "I just don't know. I—listen. How many men do you usually have there?"

"Nine are in residence now."

"All out on this job?"

"Two were out before," Mrs. Davidson said.

"Have anyone who returns call me as soon as they get back," said Merrick, "and if I'm not in call the office. If there's no answer there, call Miller at the Yard. Ask them to make sure they check on all three before they go out again."

"If there's no answer from the *office*," Mrs. Davidson breathed, as if that were a fantastic possibility.

"That's right," grunted Merrick. "Sorry. 'Bye."

The feeling of suffocation came over him again as he replaced the receiver; all of this was more alarming, because

Craigie and Loftus wouldn't have called out all the men, and gone out themselves, without telephoning him.

Would they? They'd sent him home to rest, knowing that he would have to be up and doing with the next move.

He could picture Arden's plump face.

He rang Elliott, but the other agent was out. That was as unexpected as the silent office. It was as if everyone had vanished.

He fought back fear . . .

He dialled two more places where he should find Department Z men, places which were supposed to be unknown to Arden, had been taken over since Alec had disappeared. From one, there was no answer; from the other, a middle-aged agent who was hobbling about with a foot in plaster said that the three men who had been there all night had been called out by Loftus about an hour and a half ago.

"Sure it was Loftus?" asked Merrick, abruptly.

"Didn't occur to anyone to doubt it," the other said. "Listen, Jim, you don't think—"

"I don't know what to think," Merrick said gruffly. "I'll be calling you."

He tried the office again; no one was back.

He didn't shave, but doused his face in cold water, dressed hurriedly, made one more attempt to get the Whitehall number before he left, then hurried downstairs. This time he didn't even think about Mrs. Gilmour, yet when he was in the street, something made him glance up. She was standing at her front-room window, looking out and making no attempt to conceal the fact that she was watching.

She didn't smile.

Merrick's car was in a garage nearby. He hurried to it, unlocked the door, and stepped inside.

Lying back in the car was one of Craigie's men; unconscious, or dead. And by his side was a slip of paper with a single sign, V. It was the first of these that Merrick had seen.

The feeling of suffocation almost choked him.

Then he saw that the tyres were slashed.

He half ran from the garage, telephoned a doctor from a nearby kiosk, went into Victoria Street at the double. Now he watched everyone within sight, but no one took any apparent notice of him. He fought against the feeling of suffocation and the fear which could so easily take possession of him.

There was a Department Z man in his own garage, dead or unconscious, perhaps dying.

He wasn't followed.

He hailed a taxi, said: "Scotland Yard," and sat back, but was on edge every second. He did not even feel that he could safely trust the driver, but how could Vandermin or Arden have planted a taxi just at that spot, at that time?

The taxi delivered him to Scotland Yard.

He wasn't known to many there, but flashed his card and was soon in the office of Superintendent Miller, the liaison with Department Z for as long as it had existed; a big, dusty-looking man with a forbidding stomach, mild blue eyes, a thick grey moustache but not much hair. He stood up.

He listened . . .

"I'm as worried as you are," he said. "Craigie and Loftus didn't give me any message. But whenever I call them I get that other chap, so they must have switched the line through."

"Can we get in?" Merrick asked, abruptly.

"In real emergency," Miller said, "there's one way. I'll have to have a word with my Chief. Will you wait?"

Merrick said: "Make it snappy."

The office overlooked the narrow road which led to Parliament Street before it became Whitehall, and the back of a big, grey building—which housed Craigie and Loftus. Merrick felt his breath coming quickly, painfully; much as it had done after he had been gassed at the Home.

Either Loftus and Craigie had led a raid themselves, or they had been outwitted, perhaps trapped. And they never left the office together and untenanted.

Merrick burned a cigarette away before Miller came back. The big detective was gruff and brisk moving. He took his hat from a peg, and said:

"Okay, we can go."

"How do we get in?"

"From the inside of the building," Miller said. "One of the Ministerial big shots will meet us there and open it. Surely nothing can have happened to Craigie and Loftus." His tone betrayed his fears. "I know it's a bad business, but—"

Merrick didn't speak.

They hurried out and into Parliament Street, turned and walked briskly towards the narrow street and approached the narrow door. The main entrance to the building, which they must now use, was a little way further ahead. Merrick glanced at the doorway which he usually used, saw it opening, and stopped abruptly.

"Wait a minute."

Miller stopped, and looked.

"Wait—"

The door opened wider, and Elliott limped into sight, a worried Elliott, scowling until he saw them, and then his face lit up.

"Can't get any answer," he said, limping towards them. "I don't like it a bit." Then he saw Merrick's expression, and his own changed as if he sensed the worse. "Like that, Jim?"

"Could be," Merrick said. "Will you go back to the usual door, and keep trying?"

Elliott said: "All right." His voice was strained, but he

wasn't in charge now and he took the request without the slightest hesitation. "Hell," he said, and left it at that.

Five minutes later, Merrick stood with Miller, a highly placed permanent official of the Foreign Office, and a man whom he knew to be liaison between Department Z and other branches of the Secret Service. This man removed a small electric switch, taking the outer casing away completely and, behind it, pressing a much smaller switch.

A door in this wall opened, too.

It was the back entrance to Craigie's office; an entrance known by few.

Feeling that he could hardly breathe, Merrick stepped through, behind the permanent official. He saw Craigie lying face downwards on his desk, unmoving. Otherwise the office was empty—and normal.

2 2

THE ADDRESS

Merrick reached Craigie first, but the others were with him in a moment. Craigie's body seemed limp—not cold, thank God, not cold. Merrick moved him back in the swivel armchair. That skull-like face seemed more like a death's head than ever, and the big eyes were closed, the lids were wrinkled.

There was no sign of breathing.

Merrick felt his pulse, and detected nothing; Craigie's hands were clenched tightly; he looked exactly as Iris Arden had been in her cataleptic state.

The man who served as liaison with the other secret Departments helped Merrick to move Craigie, lay him on the floor, get rugs from the corner cupboard, but only the doctors could really help. Miller was already at a telephone, calling for a doctor. The Permanent Official was looking worried and a little out of his depth.

"We might save him," the liaison officer said. That was as hopeful as anyone could put it. "Looks as if Vandermin really means to try to break the Department wide open."

Merrick grunted, then glanced again and saw the something white showing between the clenched fingers of Craigie's right hand; it might be a slip of paper. He prised the fingers open; they were warm.

A screw of paper fell from his grasp.

Merrick picked it up, as Miller finished on the telephone. All of the men stared at Merrick and he smoothed out the paper, and read:

V at Charn Lodge, Wimbledon

No one spoke.

A buzzer sounded, and Merrick looked up, saw a green light showing in the mantelpiece, and remembered that Elliott was outside. He muttered something about that, and put the slip of paper into his pocket. He found his mind working clearly again as he pressed the release button, then looked through the window into the little cubby-hole, to make sure that it was Elliott.

It was.

Elliott limped in, pasty-faced; his grey eyes seemed very bright and cold. His lips were set tightly, as if every time he put his left foot down, the ankle hurt him. It came to Merrick, then, that Elliott wouldn't be any use in any emergency; wouldn't be any good, except if he could sit down. He might take over the office, but would be no good at all on an outside job, although he'd want to be in on it.

Charn Lodge, Wimbledon, was burning itself into Merrick's mind. So were other things. Craigie would be out for hours, at best; and those hours were vital, perhaps their one remaining chance to beat Vandermin.

Someone had managed to get at Craigie, here; it looked more than ever as if Loftus and the other agents had been lured away, and wouldn't be able to raid the house. There would be just a handful of agents left, but—why use agents? It was a sickening thought, but Vandermin knew all the agents, could keep track of their movements. To catch him, people he could not know ought to be used. Craigie had implied that he no longer trusted anyone.

Elliott limped to Craigie's desk.

"So that's it," he said. "That's it. Where's Loftus?"

"Better say missing," Merrick told him what he had done, and what Arden had said. "It looks as if Arden had started moving before he talked to me. Ted—"

"Yes?" Elliott seemed unable to look away from Craigie.

"Will you take over here?"

"Doing what?"

"Taking messages, warning our chaps," Merrick said, and the need for that came to him suddenly, alarmingly; it scared him, because he ought to have thought about what else had been forgotten. "I've tried the hostel and ..." he gave the other three hide-outs. "We ought to get in touch with every other agent and warn them there might be trouble, to get away."

"Where to? What to do?" Elliott's voice was husky, as if he hardly knew what he was saying.

Merrick said: "They ought to assemble, somewhere." But the Department Z men were watched; couldn't be used; and if Elliott knew about Charn Lodge, he would want to get all the available Department men together and raid the place. Give him half a chance, and he would go to Wimbledon himself— but there was no room for crocks.

And no one could be trusted.

Not even—Loftus?

Elliott was saying: "Assemble, yes. Better not have them at different places. They'd better make sure that they're not being followed. Isn't that what Craigie would do? Have 'em make sure they're not followed, and send them to some spot where they can be called on. All together. *We must find out where these devils are!*" His voice suddenly cracked. "And where Loftus is, where the others—"

"Must have someone here to take messages and fix it with the agents who're still free," Merrick said, as if that were a new idea altogether. "You'd better do it, Ted. I—ah, here's the doctor."

Elliott turned swiftly, hopefully . . .

Elliott and a man from M.I.5 took over the office, after Craigie had been taken down to an ambulance. Merrick left with Miller and the others. No one spoke until they were out of the office. The 'back entrance' was closed, but two police guards were left outside.

The liaison officer's name was Fisher. His office was two floors above, large and spacious, with walnut panelling and a walnut desk and a large carpet. He was small, brown, wrinkled and almost bald; yet somehow didn't look an old man.

"Now what's on your mind, Merrick?" he asked, and added: "Last time I talked to Craigie, he said that Elliott was to take over in emergency; and failing Elliott, you."

It wasn't a moment for feeling satisfaction.

"And with Elliott hardly able to walk, it leaves you," went on Fisher. "Any ideas?"

Miller looked out of the window and fiddled with the most prominent button on his waistcoat.

"Yes," Merrick said, quietly. "Clear ideas. Vandermin knows all our men, and there may be more traitors. We couldn't risk using them, even if we could find them. Vandermin lets us think we're getting away with it, and then snarls at us. So we need different men. Special Branch or ordinary Yard men, anyone else you can spare are needed—all men who can't be traced through Department Z. Looks to me as if Alec Ryall or

Corlett got away with all our records, and that Vandermin has them handy," he went on. "So we want new chums."

Miller rumbled: "Seems the thing to do."

"Yes," said Fisher, more decisively, "we can use men outside the Department, but—how, exactly?"

Merrick plucked thoughts out of the confusion in his mind. He leaned heavily against the big desk as he spoke, and fiddled with his cigarette-case.

"We've got to be quick. Arden wouldn't have done what he has if it weren't important for him to stop us from doing anything quickly. He was ruffled at being driven out of the house near St. Albans. I think that there's reasonable hope that Charn Lodge is his last line of defence—that he daren't let himself be driven out of there."

"Granted, that could be," Fisher conceded.

"So we throw a cordon round Charn Lodge and the neighbourhood it's in," Merrick said. "We make sure that they can't get away. Then we close in." He hesitated. "Wait a minute," he said. "We'll need helicopters to spot the place—"

"Talking of helicopters," Fisher broke in, "the pilots of the two which were working yesterday and last night were fooled. I know the addresses which were found after the films had been developed; neither was Vandermin's or Arden's. It is fairly easy to switch cars, and that's probably what was done last night. Any idea how Craigie got this address?" He snapped his fingers. "Silly question, of course you haven't. We don't even know that it's right."

"We have to assume that it is until it's proved wrong," Merrick growled. "We'll have helicopters watching the top of the house, and a look-out kept from any high point nearby. They've used a tunnel once and might use one again, so we'll have to have a cordon spread pretty wide, and block the district completely. Anyone who leaves the enclosed area will have to be held until we can be absolutely sure that he or she isn't involved." Merrick was talking very quickly, almost to himself. "Then we have to make quite sure that it's the house we want, before we move in. We also want to try to save lives." He was thinking of Judy, of course, only of Judy; but quickly found a rational reason for saying that. "We certainly need Arden alive, Vandermin if he's there, anyone we can get our hands on. That's going to be the problem, because if we do drive them into a corner, they might commit *hara-kiri*." He didn't even smile. "I think I'll—"

The telephone-bell rang.

"Excuse me," said Fisher, and plucked the instrument up. "Fisher speaking . . . Oh, yes, hold on." He held the telephone towards Merrick. "It's Elliott."

"Thanks," said Merrick.

Everything was important, and he knew that it would be easy to jump to the wrong conclusions; but would Elliott call unless something vital were at stake?

"Hallo, Ted."

"Jim," Elliott said, in a voice which sounded so strange that for a moment Merrick wondered if it were really Elliott's. "I've heard from—Arden again."

"Oh," Merrick said heavily. "What's the ultimatum this time?"

"He says—" Elliott paused. "He has Loftus and most of our men prisoners. He says that he'll roast them alive unless we drop everything. And to prove that we mean business, he wants—"

Elliott paused again.

Merrick said: "Take it easy, Ted."

"He wants a complete list of our overseas agents and other records—in short, access to the office here. And if we don't agree—"

He didn't need to finish.

Merrick felt the gaze of the other two men on him; knew that they guessed something of what was being said. He looked out of the window, and could just see the traffic moving along Whitehall.

"In short, the complete break-up of the Department," Merrick said harshly.

"Yes," said Elliott. "Yes. Or—"

"Did he give us a time-limit?"

"Until five this afternoon," Elliott declared. "Jim, the thought's driving me crazy. What can we do? Over forty men are trapped. We can build up again with them, but without them—anyhow, it isn't a thing we can think about." He almost shouted. "He'll burn them—"

"No," Merrick said sharply. "We can't let it happen, it isn't bearable." He didn't think that, but knew that Elliott must believe that he did. They must gain time; and if Elliott were convinced that he would agree to come to terms, then he would be more convincing when Arden spoke to him again. It was quick, superficial thinking; but it seemed sound. "I'll consult the Big Shots in the Home Office and the Foreign Office, and get things moving. If Arden tackles you again, tell him that."

"If I could only do something," Elliott said harshly, "if I could get my hands round his throat—"

"Take it easy," Merrick's voice was cold. "We can't play the fool with Arden now. We can't let anything happen to Loftus and the others. It's as simple as that."

Elliott didn't answer.

"Did you hear me?" Merrick snapped.

"Yes. Yes, of course—no doubt you're right," muttered Elliott. "Believe it or not," he added with what seemed like a pathetic attempt to be flippant, "I don't feel at my best. Let me know when you've heard from the Lords High Admirals. 'Bye." He rang off.

"Proceed as arranged," Merrick said, after a long pause and while looking into Fisher's eyes. "Craigie wouldn't hesitate. We have to get Vandermin and Arden, no matter who pays for it. But before you close in, I'm going to visit them. Alone," he added. "I might be able to gain time. I'll pretend to parley, try to put them off their guard."

Neither of the others argued. No one even said that it was a forlorn hope.

23

CHARN LODGE

The house lay back from a wide residential road, within sight of Wimbledon Common. It was surrounded by a seven foot wall, and on top of the wall broken glass had been set in cement, so that small boys, cats and night marauders would have a difficult time getting over. The massive gates were of wrought iron; they had a crest on them, but Merrick didn't take any notice of that. The drive itself was smooth, and looked as if it had been freshly gravelled; there wasn't a weed to be seen. On either side were grass paths and flower beds; and the dahlias, just in flower, and zinnias and asters made a magnificent show.

It would be hard to think of anything more peaceful; more reassuring.

The gates were open. Two gardeners were at work, and they paused to look round as Merrick drove in at the wheel of his own car, with new tyres fitted.

He had an odd feeling, when he was beyond the gates; as if they might close automatically, and hem him in. He had several clear thoughts in his mind, was quite sure of what he would say to Arden; to Vandermin, if there were such a man as Vandermin.

He reached the circular carriage-way outside the front door, and felt his nervous tension increasing, could not stop himself from turning to look round.

The gates had closed.

He shivered as he got out of the car. The windows were all heavily curtained; half-way down, net curtains prevented him from seeing in. No one appeared to be looking at him. He went up the three shallow steps to the front door, which was painted deep red. The letter-box, knocker and bell were of brass, and highly polished.

He pressed the bell.

There was no immediate response. He turned and looked at the gates, and there was no doubt at all that they had closed automatically. From here the wall seemed more formidable than it had from outside.

He rang again.

He knew what to say; how to school his actions and his thoughts. He had not been followed by any Department man, by the police or by M.I.5. That had been essential to the success of the mission. If he had been followed, it was by a Vandermin man—who would have sent word ahead that Merrick was alone.

It was now nearly half-past four—half an hour to go before the expiration of Arden's ultimatum to Elliott.

He rang again, and couldn't stop himself from lighting a cigarette. So much mattered; he had come to find out where Loftus and the others were imprisoned, in the desperate hope of being able to guide rescuers to them. But even that was unimportant compared with the major purpose; to capture or to kill Arden; Vandermin; any others he found here; and Alec. Yes, if necessary, Alec—the 'kind of prisoner' who had turned traitor. That was still the thing which it was so hard to believe.

Why weren't they opening the door?

Were they waiting to see if anyone were following him?

How had they got at Craigie? How had they lured Loftus and the other men away?

Questions—

The door opened, very quietly, but he hadn't heard a sound. He started, and his heart leapt. At first all he saw was a spacious but rather gloomy hall, with a Persian carpet; then he saw a big hand, holding the door with knuckly fingers. He knew that hand.

A moment later, Kip looked at him, grinning, showing the wide, black gaps in his teeth. His face looked ruddier than ever.

"So you couldn't keep away," he sneered.

"That's right," said Merrick. He stepped inside. As he crossed the threshold, two men moved swiftly from the side of the door, he hadn't known they were there. They ran over his pockets, tapping smartly, searching for a gun or a weapon. They were slick. One man slid a hand into his trousers pocket, and brought out a pen-knife.

"Okay, take it away," Kip said.

That was all they took, for Merrick hadn't brought a gun. He had brought a weapon. It wasn't exactly a newfangled weapon but was one of the oldest known to man; and because of that, it might work where nothing else would. He knew, above everything else, that if he lost—if he saw no chance of making Vandermin and Arden prisoners, he must kill them. So in his cigarette-case were three cigarettes which were actually blow-pipes; and in each were two darts with curare on the needle-sharp tips. In South America, primitive savages had been killing their enemies with the same kind of poison and the same methods for countless years.

The hall was gloomy.

"To what do we owe this pleasure?" Kip demanded sneeringly, and turned towards the stairs. "Follow me."

Merrick obeyed; and the others brought up the rear.

The stairs were thickly carpeted, and at a half landing there was a coloured glass window; that was why it was gloomy. They reached a wide landing, and then a door which stood closed. Kip tapped; after a pause, the door seemed to open automatically.

"He's here, unarmed," Kip called.

"All right, all right, bring him in," said Arden.

So he was here.

Kip led the way, keeping very close. Merrick sensed that they half-expected him to attack Arden physically.

Arden was sitting in an easy chair, with one leg up on a pouffe. He was dressed, but wore slippers, not shoes. His back was to the window, and that put his face in shadows.

Another man, tall, very good looking, sat in another chair on the other side of the big fireplace; and he was smiling. Could he be Vandermin?

Vandermin?

Arden said: "How did you get this address, Merrick?"

Merrick said: "I've had it for some days. I've come to—" he broke off.

Vandermin—was it Vandermin? —didn't stop smiling.

"All right, tell us why you've come," said Arden testily, "and don't run away with the idea that anything will make us change our minds. Loftus and the others are in the cellar of this house, thirty-nine men altogether, and the place is soaking with petrol. One match, and that would be the end of your precious Department Z agents. If you'd had any sense you would have come to an arrangement with us in the first place, instead of making us force the issue like this."

"Well, don't blame me," Merrick said.

"What?"

"I said don't blame me."

"There's no need to be cryptic."

"I wasn't the boss," said Merrick slowly. "I am now." Everything he said had to be judged to a nicety; had to carry conviction, to put doubt into their minds. There was no certain way of being sure that it did, but he had to work on the assumption that he could do what he set out to do . . . "I'd have dealt—" he broke off, with a shrug, and took out his cigarette-case.

Kip leapt at him.

Merrick opened the case and took out a cigarette. Kip's fingers touched the case; when he took them away, there were big smears and fingerprints on the shiny gold. Merrick lit his cigarette with a lighter, and slid both case and lighter back into his pocket.

"Well, you won't do a deal now," said Arden flatly. "It's too late. You'll just do what you're told. Did you bring the records from the office?"

"No," Merrick said.

"I told you—"

"Listen," said Merrick, "I may know when I'm beaten but I'm not going to let you kill off my friends without trying to make sure that I can help them. You offered an exchange—if that isn't a deal, what is?"

Arden looked at the other man, spoke as if to an equal; perhaps a subordinate.

"What do you think, Ronny?"

Not Vandermin?

"Let him tell us why he's here," said Ronny mildly. "It won't do any harm to listen."

"Oh, all right," said Arden. "What do you think you're going to get out of this, Merrick? We know you weren't followed, but we don't know that you didn't leave the address for someone else to come to."

"No, you don't, do you?" Merrick let smoke curl from his lips. "It isn't all going your way, Arden. I can get the information you want. It will be easy. I haven't got it yet, but I can. It depends what you're going to do with it. There's one place I won't let it go to, and if you used every method of torture known to man you wouldn't get the information from me."

"Where is that one place?" Arden demanded.

Merrick said abruptly: "Moscow."

Arden shot a quick glance at Ronny; and both men smiled, as if that really amused them. Then Arden said in his off-hand way:

"That's what I've always said about Department Z, it's so out-dated as well as out-moded. Moscow, red peril, wicked Russia—that's all you seem to be able to think about. We're not agents of Moscow. We work for ourselves."

Merrick drew deeply on his cigarette; it was already burned half-way down. Kip shifted his position a little, Arden and Ronny—could he be Vandermin?—stared at Merrick, who made himself say casually:

"We'd wondered."

"Who had?" snapped Arden.

"Craigie, Loftus, the rest of us."

"What made you wonder?"

"We knew you'd got away with a lot of secret information but couldn't be sure where the stuff went," Merrick said, and told him how Craigie had reasoned. "So the obvious possibility was that you had some private row to hoe." He smiled as if it weren't really important; but his heart thumped. "And Alec Ryall's in it, is he?"

"He was easily persuaded," Arden said loftily.

Merrick felt the horror of it . . . knew how completely he had been fooled.

Corlett had been loyal.

Then Alec . . .

But Merrick had to keep up his pretence; still had his part to play.

"And Corlett."

Arden gave a queer, twisted smile. The other man laughed.

"Oh, no," Arden said. "Not Corlett. He was loyal to you. We needed a scapegoat, and he was just the man. We worked on him all the time, to help distract attention from the agent who was betraying you. Then Craigie rested him, but he tried to work on his own and we had to hold him. You really killed Corlett, Merrick."

And that was true. He had never doubted Corlett's crookedness because he had never liked the man. He had killed Corlett.

"Why don't you try to persuade me?" Merrick asked savagely.

Arden moved his hands, an impatient gesture, rather as if he were brushing some ridiculous idea away.

"It's too late. You should have brought those papers. We can't be sure we can trust you to go back and get them." He said that as if he thought it might be possible to use Merrick; and all Merrick needed now was time. Arden had twice fooled him into thinking there was no urgency. If he could convince Arden that no raid was planned, then the coming raid would have a better chance to succeed.

"Merrick," said Ronny, speaking, taking the initiative for the first time, "how did you get this address?"

Merrick said brusquely: "I got it, never mind how."

"Oh, but we do mind," said Ronny, and he stood up slowly.

Of course he cared; it was vital for them to know; Merrick had been waiting for them to force that question. "How did you get it?"

Merrick said: "Craigie had it."

"That's a lie," Ronny said softly.

"Oh, no," said Merrick. He put his hand to his pocket again, and although they knew that he had been searched, Kip and one of the others moved nearer; evidence of their state of nerves. Everyone here was nervous—waiting. For what?

Merrick took out the slip of paper.

"He was lying across his desk. This was in his hand. Judging from the scrawl, he'd just received a telephone message and scribbled the address down—and then collapsed. How did you get at him?"

Arden took the slip of paper and Ronny joined him; they read it together. And again Merrick knew that they were nervous, that there was something they didn't understand. What frightened them?

"How could Craigie get it?" Arden demanded, as if he expected an answer to come out of the air. "I don't understand, I thought—"

He broke off.

The telephone bell rang at the instrument close to his side. He snatched it up, Merrick felt a fierce excitement, for this was the first time he had seen fear in Arden's eyes.

"Arden here . . . Oh, yes, yes." A note of relief came quickly. "Listen, Van, Craigie discovered this address before he collapsed, Merrick's here now . . . Yes, Merrick . . . But surely you knew he was coming . . . My goodness, did he fool you? . . . Don't you know whether he's arranged for others to come? I— good gracious!" On Arden's lips the remark was almost ludicrous; but the thing that did Merrick good was Arden's new flood of alarm; there was alarm on Ronny's face, too. "My dear

Van, you'd better come over right away, get here as soon as you can, in case we've run into trouble. . . . Yes, hurry! All right, Van."

He banged down the receiver.

Merrick thought: 'Van for Vandermin?'

And Arden had been sure that Vandermin had all-seeing eyes, was shocked beyond words to know that he hadn't realised that Merrick had the address.

"Van's coming," Arden said, superfluously. "And for safety's sake we'd better be ready to get away then, Ronny. That's if we can't make Merrick tell us everything."

"Bring Judy Ryall up here," suggested Ronny. "She'll help us to make him talk."

Merrick clenched his teeth and clenched his hands at the same time.

Arden said: "No, we'll take him downstairs. Let's go." He stretched out for the stick, grabbed it, then got up, grunting when he put his weight on his sound leg and his stick. "I owe you something for this leg of mine, Merrick," he said vexedly. "I would get a lot of pleasure out of seeing you suffer, but I'm not vindictive, if you're a sensible fellow, no one need get hurt. Not even Judy Ryall!"

Did he know how that slashed across Merrick's mind?

They went out, Kip bringing up the rear, almost treading on Merrick's heels.

24

VANDERMIN

Arden limped down the stairs ahead of the others, turned alongside the foot of the stairs, then went through a door beneath the stairs. Ronny followed, the men who had greeted Merrick at the house went next; then Merrick; then Kip; and Kip was still almost treading on Merrick's heels. The passage beyond was narrow and gloomy.

Wright slipped ahead of Arden, and opened a door.

They went in.

Merrick stepped inside, and then stopped abruptly. His heart raced. He felt as he had several times before, when seeing Judy, but this time it was worse.

She was chained to a ring in the wall of the room.

There she stood, breathtakingly beautiful, quite still and somehow proudly. The chain led from the ring to a leather belt at her waist. She had fair room to move about. In the room was a single bed, a wash-basin, an easy chair, some books and magazines.

One wall was of glass.

Judy saw Merrick. Her composure weakened for a

moment; she caught her breath. But she tightened her lips quickly, and looked at Arden.

"Friend of yours come to see you," Arden said offhandedly. "Push that stool up for me, Kip." He waited while Kip obeyed, then sat down heavily, sticking his wounded leg straight out. "Remember Mrs. Ryall, Merrick?" That was a sneer, but Arden wasn't very serious about it. "Understand you became very good friends at the chalet in Switzerland, that you're quite fond of her. Well, we don't want to hurt her for the sake of it. Up to you. Bones can be broken very easily, and they hurt."

Merrick felt as if the air had turned icy cold.

"Don't you like the idea?" asked Arden. "These emotions! Just tell me, what real difference would it make if she were to have her cheeks branded? Eh? It would hurt for a bit, but afterwards she wouldn't feel anything, just have a few scars. That wouldn't make any difference to your affections, would it, Merrick?" The casual sneer came again.

Merrick said: "Judy, where's Alec?"

She said: "He's not here, Jim, he's never been here. He *is* dead."

Merrick watched her, as if through mists of bitter tears.

"When I talked to you on the telephone, that beast was standing over me, with a knife in his hand," she said, and looked at Kip with eyes which held all the contempt in the world. "He would have—oh, it doesn't matter. Arden told me what to say."

Merrick said: "Yes, of course." He turned to Arden. He had to remember that for the time being he must be all sweet reasonableness. Time, time, time! "What did it matter if I thought that Alec was dead?"

"Forget it," said Arden. "I wanted to impress you with the importance of the message, didn't I? And to stop you from worrying too much about what was happening. That was when Loftus and the others were walking into my parlour."

"Cellar," murmured Ronny, and smiled.

"Don't be facetious," Arden rebuked. "Merrick, I want to know how you got this address. You know more than you've told us, and I also want to know what plans you laid before you came here. I don't believe that you came just of your own free will, to try to battle this out on your own. Oh, no! That doesn't make sense, and isn't consistent with your usual behaviour. You've been disciplined to consult others. You don't work on your own. Come here a minute."

His back was to the long glass window wall.

Merrick joined him.

He could see into the cellar; a crowded one, filled with agents, most of them sitting awkwardly, resignedly. He knew many of the men. Loftus was talking to a man whom Merrick didn't know.

"Now, how did you find out about this address, and whom else did you tell?" asked Arden, in his most hectoring voice.

"Craigie had it," Merrick answered quietly. "I don't know who telephoned it to him. I've told no one else."

"That's a story I don't believe." Arden glanced at Kip, who moved away from Merrick, as if he could anticipate the orders which were about to come. "We haven't much time, Kip," he said quite casually, "better start with her fingers. Get ready. Merrick, I want the truth and all the truth—and if you lie again, Mrs. Ryall will soon be nursing one broken finger. And if you keep lying—"

"I tell you it's the truth!"

"I don't believe it." Arden waved his hand impatiently. "Why are you such a fool, Merrick? You've all been the same, you don't seem to think that I've any intelligence at all. But look at my record—mine and Vandermin's. You shouldn't need telling that we've successfully outwitted you all along. It's no small thing, you know, to be able to make a laughing stock of a Department like yours. Only brilliant men could do it—brilliant men with a little inside help, of course! Do you know, Merrick, some of the most brilliant spies in the world are in our employ—very brave men, too. The real spies, the important operatives, not the ordinary little agents who pick up a trifle here and a trifle there—but the big fish. And when we found that Department Z was becoming a nuisance, we simply decided to get control of it. Vandermin did that—he'll be here soon."

Merrick hardly heard him.

Merrick was staring at Judy, who was standing so erect; and at the man named Kip, whose lips were parted in that ugly grin, and who held her wrist in his left hand, and her little finger in his right—as if he would force it up at a word from Arden.

Merrick could imagine the crack as the bone broke.

Arden went on in his hectoring way: "So why try to fool men of our calibre, Merrick? It's just a waste of time. What's the point, anyway? You seemed worried about Moscow, but we don't work for Moscow, we work for ourselves. We won't put Great Britain or the Commonwealth in any danger—at least we won't if the Governments take a sensible view. We've collected all this secret information and still have it, we're prepared to sell it back to the Governments. That's straightforward enough, isn't it? We'll sell it back, guaranteeing not to double—sell to any other country. And don't ask what guarantee you have—you'd find out if another country had the first lot, and wouldn't pay up for more. It's in our own interests to be straightforward about it, and Vandermin is quite definite about that. We've all the different formulæ and documents here, and when we know that there's no danger of our being found and identified, we'll start dealing. You can be the first intermediary, if you behave yourself. Have you made arrangements for the house to be raided, or haven't you? Who else knows the address?"

He glanced at Judy.

Merrick didn't answer but gritted his teeth and looked away from the girl—and then took out the cigarette-case.

He couldn't use it, yet. He had to wait for Vandermin. He had to be sure that he could kill all the leaders. Vandermin—Arden—Ronny. And if he could kill Kip too, that would be wonderful; there wasn't anyone else in the world he wanted to kill more than that ugly brute.

"I'll ask you once more," breathed Arden. "Who—"

Then the door opened.

Elliott came in.

"Why, hallo, Van," Arden said. "You've been quick."

A moment before, it would have seemed impossible to forget Judy and the brute who was holding her hand and her finger. But Merrick did forget her; forgot everything in the wave of disbelief that came with the sight of Elliott, and with Arden's matter-of-fact greeting.

"Why, hallo, Van." That was to *Elliott.*

Gradually, the shock effect subsided; Merrick could make himself think again, but it was still about Elliott. He looked at the man, who didn't limp much now, but twisted his moustache in a way which was almost second nature.

"'Lo, Josh," he said. "'Lo, Malcolm. What's happening? Oh, I see." He turned to Merrick. "Must be quite a shock. Why didn't you tell me you were coming here?"

He was very matter-of-fact, and that helped Merrick to keep steady beneath the weight of bitterness at his own blind folly. He had disliked Corlett, and readily, almost eagerly, suspected him. He had liked Elliott, and seen him as a typical

Department man, never given a serious thought to the possibility that he was disloyal.

"Merrick is being stubborn and foolish," Arden said. "But he's squeamish about us hurting Mrs. Ryall."

Merrick stood still, silent.

"Jim, talk quick," said Elliott brusquely. "Did you know I was on the other side? Does Miller know?"

Merrick didn't speak.

"Does Miller know this address?" Elliott moved forward a hand raised. Anger and fear were growing in him, and that was good to see.

Arden said: "Let's get out, let's—"

"We won't run until we know we have to," Elliott said, "there's a fortune in this house, remember. But we'll soon know what's cooking. Talk, Merrick. If you don't, you'll see Judy writhing, hear her screaming." He meant that; his flat voice made the threat sound deadly. "Is Miller on his way here?"

Merrick thought: 'I mustn't tell him.' But he knew that he would have to if they began to torture Judy.

"Start it, Kip," said Arden, breathlessly. "Hurry!"

"Merrick, *talk*," Elliott rapped.

There was a moment's pause; a hurtful tension.

Then Kip dropped Judy's hand.

That was so utterly unexpected that everyone stared at him. He just let her hand fall. Then he put his own hand to his pocket and drew out an automatic pistol.

"You'll burn them up whatever Merrick says," he said. "The answer is no, we won't talk. Nice work, Merrick—when will the raid start? You couldn't have failed to fix one, could you?—not after I telephoned Craigie with this address this morning. Name of Herrington, Kip only to my enemies," he added brightly.

Kip—a Department Z man. *Kip.*

Time seemed to stand still.

Arden said hoarsely: "So—it's you. Van, I knew there was a leakage when your warning about the raid on Red Walls wasn't delivered. *He* must—"

"Yes, I took that message," Kip said, "and forgot to pass it on. I—"

Then Elliott, *alias* Vandermin, hurled himself at him.

25

A MAN NAMED HERRINGTON

Elliott leapt and Kip fired. Elliott staggered when he was a yard from Kip, but Arden's hand was also at his pocket. So was Ronny's. Merrick did the one thing he could do without equal. From a standing start, he reached Arden and cracked a fist under his chin, then turned on to Ronny. Ronny had a gun out, his finger was on the trigger, his eyes blazed.

Merrick hit him.

The shot roared as Ronny staggered away. Then Merrick was at his throat, hands squeezing, choking the life out of him. Ronny gasped and tried to struggle but hadn't the strength. His body sagged. Merrick flung him away and turned towards the others. Kip, his smile strangely different, had a nasty wound in his cheek. He was standing by Judy, holding a key in his hand. Arden was on the floor, and looked as if he were unconscious or dead; the other two men who had come in with Kip were lying in huddled heaps.

Kip said: "If we get a move on, Merrick, we'll set Loftus free before anyone in the house realises that anything's wrong. Have you planned a raid?"

"They're waiting until five-thirty," Merrick said hoarsely. "Police and—never mind. I can't see you—"

"As a hero," Kip said and grinned; he looked almost grotesque. "Nor can Judy!" He turned the key and the leather belt fell from her waist, the chain clanked against the wall. She stared at him as if she couldn't believe that this thing was real. "Judy," went on Kip, "I'm more sorry than you'll ever know that I had to scare you the way I did. When I nearly strangled you I hated myself. But I had to keep in with Arden and Wright. I just had to wait until I knew where the headquarters were—and the time came to tell Craigie."

He paused.

The men below didn't know that anything had gone wrong; they could be seen but couldn't see. Loftus was leaning back against the wall with his eyes closed; tired, probably despairing.

"Let's get out," Kip said. "We needn't worry about this lot, we can lock 'em in. There are a dozen other men in the house, including three guards at the cellar. Judy, you'll have to wait where we tell you."

"Anything you say," she said.

Kip grinned, and seemed eager to talk.

"That's something to hear! I wasn't a big shot, mind you. At first I worked for Wright, knowing he was one of them, but I wasn't promoted for a long time. I knew there was a man named Arden, but wasn't assigned to him until a few months ago. I tipped Craigie off whenever I could, but the main thing was to make the mob feel quite sure that they could trust me. It wasn't until last night that I discovered this was the main headquarters. I had a lot of trouble telephoning Craigie, but got through in time. If Elliott had doped him half an hour earlier—"

He didn't finish, and was moving as he talked, as if the words came bubbling out of him, and couldn't be held back.

Merrick said: "Elliott," as if he were dreaming. "I suppose I'll get used to it."

"Yes," Kip said. "He made one mistake—thought that Craigie and Loftus told him everything, whereas they were the only two men who knew that I'd got in with the Vandermin gang. Some things I can prove," he went on gustily. "It really was a private racket, the idea was to sell formulæ and secrets back to various Governments. Don't ask me whether it would have come off, I don't know—but I think it would. There were other angles, too. They could play one country off against another, and work on commercial interests, too. It could have become quite a business."

They were nearing the door which led under the stairs into the hall. He stopped speaking at last. He held up a hand to tell them to stay where they were. They stood quite still. He went into the hall and beckoned them a moment later.

They followed him.

"Here, Judy," Kip said, and opened the door of a small cloakroom. "Lock yourself in. Don't open the door for anyone but Merrick or me."

"All right," Judy said. She went into the cloakroom; a moment later, Merrick heard the key turn in the lock.

"Now we've both got guns," Kip whispered. "Won't be long. Of course, Elliott saw the danger to the organization—knew it would come from Department Z, so he just set out to smash it. Could tell you a thing or two. He blew up Red Walls, by the way—made you think we had. He'd got everything laid on and there wasn't much he missed, but apparently he missed the fact that you'd started to work on your own. Subconscious suspicion of him, I wonder?"

"No." Merrick could have giggled. "I didn't trust him with a weak ankle! I knew he'd want to be in it with everything he'd got. Well, I thought I knew."

They were in the kitchen; it was empty. The approach to the cellar was from another small room. They reached it without trouble. Kip saw the first of the guards, and went down to see him briskly. He didn't need to use a gun, just knocked him out.

It was ludicrously easy—

Merrick made Kip open the door, made him go through first, and was satisfied to see the expression on the faces of the Department agents; on Loftus's, too. He realised then that Loftus had given up hope.

"Too bad that you all won't need rescuing when the real squad arrives," said Kip, still bursting with words. "All over, Bill, and all clear!"

Merrick did not know everything until a week later; he learned it item by item, a little here, a little there.

Many things had happened in that week.

Craigie had recovered. It was now known that Elliott had been doping him over a long period—to break down his will-power. In the end Elliott had scratched him with a glass needle infected with cataleptic serum. Had he not been rushed to hospital, Craigie would have died.

Everything had been done to draw suspicion and attention away from Elliott; but now all the missing papers had been found, together with evidence that it had been a 'private' venture. Ronny, the third in command, had made a full confession, although neither Arden nor Elliott would say a word. Disappointed, warped fascists, anarchists, all social misfits, had been forged into a powerful, daring group. There was already seventeen prisoners; more would be taken day by day.

It was through Ronny that the Department learned most of

the answers. The personality of Vandermin had been built up into a legendary one. Elliott had been the first actually to use the name; and it had become his nickname.

The plot had started years ago when Arden had bribed Elliott to give away a trifle of information. The advantage to spies of having access to Department Z information had been obvious. Elliott had worked hard to get a place in the hierarchy of the Department, but sooner or later suspicion was bound to fall on an agent; so the plan to incriminate Corlett had been built up. Then when Alec Ryall had been seriously wounded and taken away, a new idea had been conceived—to have Craigie suspecting both Alec and Corlett. To succeed it had to look as if Alec were alive. 'Vandermin' and Arden had set out to do that, very cleverly.

Judy's kidnapping had been to put the finishing touch to the deception.

Elliott had planned to take over control of the Department completely, but in order to, had to keep himself absolutely free from suspicion. Hence his 'warning' at Red Walls; and his reason for giving Arden away at the Home—knowing that he could make sure that Arden and the other men would escape. To the last it had been made to appear that Elliott could not be involved; even Arden's demand for the list of overseas agents had helped to draw suspicion away from Elliott.

At every step, Elliott had planned to discredit other Department agents, too.

Once Alec Ryall was a prisoner and a suspect traitor, Merrick had become important. As a close friend of Ryall, suspicion could easily be slanted his way. Through Iris, it had been planned to put him unconscious with the cataleptic serum, kidnap him, and then strengthen the idea that the two friends had become renegades.

At the Nursing Home, Arden had decided not to use

Merrick that way, and had risked killing him; but he had not taken a risk with Judy. He had wanted her alive, a foil for spreading the conviction that Alec Ryall was alive.

The serum was a by-product of research work being carried out in foreign countries—'Vandermin' had stolen samples and used it sparingly. The gas which had so affected Merrick, nearly killing him, was from a similar source.

Other things became clear.

'Kip' Herrington had been Craigie's one trump, but he had not been really close to the heart of affairs until the last few days. He had not known about Charn Lodge, or Elliott, or the truth about Alec until the last minute. But he had discovered a little at a time; long before the others, Craigie had known that Alec was dead; and the probability that Kip would be able to break Vandermin from the inside had given Craigie the confidence which had once cheered Merrick up.

When the final showdown had drawn near, Elliott had planned a master-stroke of great simplicity. He used a new Department code word to send all the agents to a house near Charn Lodge; and they had walked one by one into a trap. Loftus had gone to another rendezvous to meet some agents, and been easily overpowered.

There was nothing else that Merrick really needed to know. Yet he talked to Craigie, who was well on the mend, to Loftus, Kip and Judy, about Alec. He had been quite right in believing that Alec had been fatally wounded when he had seen him from the roof. Judy hadn't believed it, simply because she hadn't wanted to.

She had been kidnapped as part of the plot to convince the Department that Alec was alive and a traitor. The build-up to the kidnapping, the letter which she had thought was from Alec, had all had the same purpose. Once at Red Walls, she had realised that Alec was dead. Under pressure, she had telephoned Merrick.

"Which made us feel sure Alec was dead," Merrick said.

"Motives don't matter much now," Judy sounded weary.

They were in her flat, at Barnes. She was moving to a smaller one, in Town, and Merrick was helping her to pack. The removal van would soon be here, and there was little left to do.

It was over four months since they had first met here; since Alec had come on the point of death, making a sacrifice which had so nearly been wasted. Merrick wondered what was really in her mind, how desperately she felt about Alec. He loved her with a quieter passion now; knew that he would love her for always; that was a simple thing to be accepted without question. But when to tell her again, if in fact she needed telling, and when to believe that there might be cause to hope, he didn't know.

He drove her to her new flat—with its large living-room, small bedroom, tiny kitchen and a bathroom that was absurdly cramped.

"Leave me on my own now, Jim," Judy begged. "I'd rather be, for a bit. But call me soon."

He took her hands.

"I'll call you whenever you like," he said, "now, or in a year, in five years, ten. You know what I mean."

"I know," she said, and her smile told him that there would be a day when she would forget that she was a kind of prisoner of the past, and when she would walk with him in the freedom of the present.

ABOUT THE AUTHOR

John Creasey, born in 1908, was a paramount English crime and science fiction writer who used myriad pseudonyms for more than six hundred novels. He founded the UK Crime Writers' Association in 1953. In 1962, his book *Gideon's Fire* received the Edgar Award for Best Novel from the Mystery Writers of America. Many of the characters featured in Creasey's titles became popular, including George Gideon of Scotland Yard, who was the basis for a subsequent television series and film. Creasey died in Salisbury, UK, in 1973.

DEPARTMENT Z

FROM OPEN ROAD MEDIA

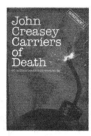
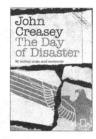

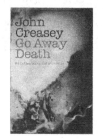

OPEN  ROAD

INTEGRATED MEDIA

OPEN ROAD
INTEGRATED MEDIA